WHISKEY TANGO FOXTROT

ACES HIGH MC - DAKOTAS
BOOK 2

CHRISTINE MICHELLE

ABOUT THE BOOK

A tattoo artist and biker named Tango came to save the day when my brother put my life in danger again.

Stupid name.

Sexy biker.

Unfortunately for me, he seemed to be in a weird relationship with his buddies Whiskey, Fox, and their girl Amy.

There was no way I would sign on to be the lettuce in that screwed up multi-partner-sandwich.

Nope. Nope. Nope.

I might need protection from his entire MC, but I absolutely would not share my man.

From the moment I laid eyes on Liza, I knew she was the one.

Protecting her quickly became a personal matter rather than another job for the club.

Loving her would be so easy. If only my past, and the screwed-up relationship my friends attempted to drag me into, hadn't become a problem.

- MC Romance
- Romantic Suspense
- Small Town Romance
- Friends to Lovers
- Other Woman Drama
- Devoted Hero

TRIGGER WARNINGS

- Strong Language
- Violence
- Assault
- Death of a loved one
- Other woman drama
- Multi-person relationships (not main characters)
- Sexual situations written on page
- Alcohol and drug mentions
- Attempted baby trapping (not by main character)
- More potential triggers not listed here.

AHMC

DAKOTAS

2

Tango & Liza

PROLOGUE

"WHAT. THE. FUCK." THE BLOND DUDE, WITH THE PATCH THAT
listed his name as Rabbit, laughed as he called out those
three words that apparently meant more to him than they
did to us. The three of us stared at him as if he'd lost his
damn mind. He hadn't said it in a questioning way. The idiot
was full-on belly laughing. Then he sobered, looked at us like
we were the crazy ones for not getting his joke, and shook his
head.

"You don't get it? Come on! I can't be the only one to have
pointed it out to you guys. You've been together how long?"

"We've known each other eight years," Waters, one of my
two best friends who flanked my right side, explained. The
three of us met in Army basic training and managed to stick
together for the entirety of our military careers. That was not
always an easy feat, but we managed, thanks to our special-
izations.

"I'm not getting what's so fuckin' funny," Farley grumbled to the man from my left side.

I

Rabbit started pointing at us in succession. "Waters, Travers, and Farley. Dudes, you're even lined up perfectly in a row." We were still giving him blank face as he slapped a hand over his own mug and dragged it down his cheeks incredulously. Then he glanced at each of us in turn as he stated, "W," while pointing at Waters. His accusatory finger moved in my directions while calling out, "T". Then he slid his attention to Farley as he guffawed through saying the letter, "F".

It finally dawned on me, as literally every man and woman in the clubhouse began laughing at our expense.

"What. The. Fuck." Rabbit called out again, slowly this time, as to leave no doubt what he meant, for our benefit. "Seriously? I'm the first to call the three of you on that in eight fuckin' years?" We all shrugged at once, which apparently was hilarious to the men around us.

"They have my vote as long as they get to be Whiskey, Tango, and Foxtrot once they make it through their prospecting period," Rabbit laughed as he made the proclamation to his club brothers.

"Fuck that!" Farley was the grumpiest bastard ever to be put on this planet. "The fuck if I'm rolling out with an old bitty dance as my fucking name, phonetic alphabet be damned."

Rabbit waved away his concern. "No worries, we can shorten it to Fox, dude."

That was the day the boys and I became prospects for the Aces High Motorcycle Club, and the day we received our three-part moniker. We would forever on be collectively known as WTF, or What The Fuck, but separately we became

Whiskey, Tango, and Fox thanks to the first initial in each of our last names and our Army service fucking us over phonetically.

1. MEMBERS GET BENEFITS
TANGO - 1 YEAR, 3 MONTHS, AND
1 WEEK AGO

"Calm your asses down! I know some of you need to get home to your families today, it being Christmas and all, but we had a special announcement and celebration that couldn't wait. We're being cheap and combining Club Christmas with an Induction Ceremony. We'll do a big blowout and invite other chapters after the holidays, but for now, Whiskey, Tango, and Fox, get your asses up here!" Iceman shouted

"Did you know this was coming?" Whiskey asked me. I took a minute to appreciate the fact that I was thinking of Waters as Whiskey now too. I just shook my head as we moved up to the stage that was sometimes used for the dancers who came by for special events.

"It's been nine months of prospecting for you guys, and a few more of you three ugly fuckers hanging around before that," Rage, the club's Vice President, yelled into the crowd as we all hopped up on the fairly low stage set in the corner of the commons area of the Dakotas Chapter clubhouse.

"Today, we are giving birth to fucking triplets! Welcome to Aces High gentlemen. You've each earned permanent membership with us." He held out a brand-new leather Kutte that had Whiskey's name over the left side of the chest. Then he turned it over and we all saw the Aces High MC rocker at the top, the smoking skull with the top hat and four Aces from a deck of cards below it. Beneath that was the bottom rocker that stated we were members of the Dakotas Chapter.

Whiskey took his Kutte and flicked it on without missing a beat while Rage held mine up and I took it with fucking pride. Fox was next, and while he hesitated slightly, he beamed with pride the minute the leather vest settled on his big, broad shoulders. A round of cheers went up when we all had our kuttes on. Iceman and Rage came over to shake each of our hands and then they pounded their fists over the rocker with our name on our chests. Sometime during the night, every single full member of the Aces High MC who were present pounded their fist into our name tapes as well.

Luckily, the shots we were given rivaled the punches, and by the end of the night when we should have been sore as fuck, we were all numb to the pain and flying high on our new position while being drowned in alcohol.

It was, hands down, one of the most amazing nights of my life, even if the morning was coincidentally one of the worst hangovers I've ever experienced. The wakeup wasn't exactly normally either. I knew right away that I wasn't in the house we had all shared during our prospecting period.

Instead, I was in what appeared to be a hotel room with a bed, utilitarian dresser across form where I had been sleeping, and then a door that must have led to a bathroom or closet. I attempted to sit up, but there was a solid thigh across my mid-section and someone's arm had me locked down on the mattress that suddenly seemed to contain far too many limbs. I lifted my head and glanced around to see that the arm across my chest belonged to Whiskey who was facing the other direction, toward Fox, who was damn near falling off the bed. Down by my feet, was a feminine body and the source of the thigh that was currently draped across my middle and so that her feet were resting on Whiskey's back.

I noticed some blonde hair and a strange fish tattoo on what looked like someone's shoulder. That triggered a memory. Lips wrapped around my dick, my hands fisted in blonde hair, staring down at that tattoo and wondering why it was there as Whiskey nailed the girl from behind and Fox was busy sucking on her clit while all that was going on. Jesus. I'd never had such a vivid flashback in my life. I'd never shared a woman with anyone before either. I hoped like hell that all I received was that remembered blow job. Whiskey, Fox, and I were close, but I didn't know how well those friendships would remain intact if I found out that anything else had gone down between the three of us – me specifically.

I glanced back over to my side noting that Whiskey and Fox were both a tangle of limbs on the other side of the bed, and then I glanced down remembering the masculine arm that was draped over me as well as the feminine legs. Hmm, I guess at least that part didn't bother me as much as I thought it would.

I attempted to dislodge the bodies that held me in place, because I had to piss, and my mouth was stuck together in a nasty tequila and beer film that wasn't going to clear itself without the aid of a toothbrush and toothpaste. Before I managed to get out from under the leg, the owner of said leg grumbled, "Where you goin', sexy?" She hadn't even looked up from where her face was still buried in the blanket that was bunched up under my feet at the bottom of the bed we were had all crashed in.

"Bathroom, move!" I managed to get out even as the alcohol still ruminating in my belly threatened reemergence. Instead of moving, the woman – whoever she was – giggled and decided to slide further on top of me, locking my lower legs in with her upper body.

"I didn't get to enjoy you properly last night, baby. I want to feel that thick cock of yours in more than just my mouth."

"That's not happening, now move, or the only thing you'll be getting from my dick is some fresh, hot piss!" That was probably uncalled for, and usually I didn't treat women like shit, even after having one stomp all over my heart previously, but I was in a serious state, and she was hindering my ability to go get myself under control.

"No need to be cranky!" Said the crankiest fucker of all of us as Whiskey laughed at Fox as he called me out. Fox tossed a pillow at my head, and Whiskey was wise enough to remove his arm from my chest and keep his mouth shut about it.

"Just go piss and bring back some water. I feel like I've been back in the desert for a week, and I ran out of drink three days ago." He smacked his dry lips together, making a think and nasty noise as he did so as if to reiterate just how badly he needed some water.

"Jesus," I muttered while flinging the woman's legs off my body. I hadn't overdone it like last night in a long damn time. I glanced over and picked up my kutte. It was the reason we all went as wild as we had last night after becoming official patched members of the Aces High MC. We had all three left the military behind for our own reasons, but it was clear we needed a brotherhood still. These guys were it, and I was happier than hell that we'd found them when we did, because I'd been sinking, and Whiskey and Fox knew it, too. The club gave me a purpose that kept me above water when I didn't really care if I sank or not.

I swallowed thickly, remembering all that we'd fought through to get home, all the brothers we'd lost, and then to have Camilla's betrayal top everything. I shook off and tried to find some toothpaste to get the foul taste of the night before out of my mouth. We must have ended up in one of the club girl's rooms, considering all the feminine shit all over the counter space.

I gave up when I couldn't find what I was looking for and moved back into the other room. The blonde was riding Whiskey while Fox was riding the blonde. Whiskey noticed me standing there and grinned over at me.

"Plenty of room, brother," he groaned as the woman must have done something with that swivel of her hips to elicit the response. Then he tapped her lips as if directing me to the third unused hole the woman possessed. I sighed and moved to set the glass of water I'd brought him down on the nightstand. Then I moved toward the other door across the room from the bed.

"Aw, don't go. I didn't get a chance to feel that giant cock of yours inside me." Her words were barely audible over the moans as she was double penetrated by my two best friends.

"And you never will," I answered before tipping my chin up at my brothers and sliding through the open door. "We still in the clubhouse?"

"Yeah, man." I nodded at Fox's quick response, having figured as much. Some of the BRATs – bitches relinquishing ass and tits – as the guys here so cleverly nicknamed them, were allowed to stay at the clubhouse in their own wing. It was fucking convenient when you thought about it.

The guys all had a stable of willing and available pussy to drop into when they needed a release, and none of that pussy had strings attached to it. The women got their bad boy fix, a place to stay, and their college paid for if they wanted to go. It was a win-win for everyone who wanted to participate. I didn't feel like participating any more than I already had.

"Hey man, you guys have a good night?" Rabbit asked as he left another room just down the hall while zipping his pants up.

I tipped my head to indicate the room I'd just left. "The other guys are still having a good night," I answered with a grin on my face that felt more like a grimace as my head pounded to a fucking death metal drummer's beat.

Rabbit laughed at me and then clapped a hand on my shoulder. "Come on. A greasy breakfast will do you some good. You look like hell man." He rubbed the side of his own temple. "Probably shouldn't have killed that bottle of tequila with you last night. Shit, brother, I feel about as bad as you look."

"Thanks," I managed to groan as we moved through the hall and off toward the kitchen. I could already smell the bacon frying, and my queasy stomach growled in protest that I hadn't already putting some of the greasy, salty goodness in my mouth. Rabbit waited to give me the third degree until I'd managed to wolf down some eggs, bacon, and sausage gravy with biscuits. The gravy probably hadn't been a wise choice, but I couldn't resist. It was one of the few things I missed from Army life.

"Why aren't you in there still enjoying your night? That was a hell of a party last night. I know you you're your boys were still lingering with Sherry-Baby, but why aren't you?" Rabbit started the coffee pot so that he could brew a stronger pot. That was something I noticed him doing often. No one else wanted to drink the sludge he made, so he mostly had it all to himself until he finished the pot or someone else came along and dumped the sludge out.

I shrugged. "Woke up feeling like a truck ran me over, some bitch sprawled across my body wanted to play games and not let me up to take a piss until I insulted her," I grumbled. "Then the guys were double teaming her when I came out of the bathroom. That shit just isn't my scene as a sober man. Honestly, I'm shocked that I went there as a drunk."

Rabbit laughed. "I get that. I've never been good with sharing either."

"You were still in one of those rooms."

"Yeah, but I'm not marrying that pussy, and I'm not dicking it at the same time someone else is either," he stated before shoving another piece of toast in his mouth. "I don't go there often with the club women," he explained, even though he almost seemed embarrassed to admit it. "I think they're a lot more trouble than their time is worth, but every now and then, I kill a bottle of tequila with a friend and make stupid ass decisions."

A redheaded woman had just walked in as he was saying that, and she apparently took offense, because I watched as her eyes began to well up with tears just before she turned and stomped off. My attention on her had Rabbit glancing over his shoulder too. He let out a long sigh, and then just shrugged his shoulders.

"Better she knows that now than her trying to catch feelings that will never be returned. These women don't get it. They're here as convenient pussy. Almost no one marries convenient pussy." He pointed to where the girl had just left the room. "That's exactly why, too. They think they're going to get a proposal or something. The guys here who get mixed up in the marriage and old lady business marry the ones that all their brothers haven't had their dicks in yet." I didn't disagree with that sentiment. I wasn't sure how I'd feel knowing that all my club brothers had been with my woman.

"The thing is, most of them understand that, and they're just here to get the bills paid and have a good time while they can, you know? But there's no process to be able to weed out all the ones who are secretly hoping to land an old man."

"I get where that could be a problem."

"We try to keep the drama with the BRATs down in this chapter. That means when one of them catches feelings, and those feelings aren't reciprocated, we usually let them go. If it ever becomes a problem for you, Whiskey, or Fox just let us know and we'll take care of shit.

"Nah, man. I'm straight. I won't ever be with any of them enough to allow those feelings to develop."

"I heard you don't fuck women, that true?" he eyed me oddly as he asked the question.

"Yeah, I guess so."

"What's up with that?"

"Exactly what we've been talking about. I can get a blow job that takes the edge off, give them nothing, and then no feelings develop."

"Damn, dude, that's kind of cold."

"No, it's just honest. I don't want anything from any of them. If they offer up something, and don't get what they want, someone else will be there to help them out. I trusted a woman with my heart and body before. That shit didn't turn out well for me. When I feel the need to release some tension, I blow and go."

Rabbit laughed at the way I presented it. "Blow and go!" He chuckled harder for a minute before sobering. "I guess it's more like the blow and then you go."

"I like to keep it simple."

Rabbit nodded his head sagely before spitting out a hard truth. "Eventually, you're going to get over that bitch of an ex of yours fuckin' you over the way she did. When you do, it'll be because a woman you can't look away from walked through the door." I noticed his attention moved to Charlie, the woman who had become our Vice President's old lady recently.

"Great party last night, Tango. Congrats on becoming a full member!" The woman in question called over to me as she wiped sleep from her eyes and headed for the dreaded coffee pot of sludge.

"Thanks, Charlie."

Rage was quick on her heels sweeping in behind her, locking his arms around her waist and making his woman giggle. The minute he scooped her up in his arms and whispered something in her ear that made her cheeks and ears turn red, Rabbit looked away.

"That a problem for you?"

"Nah, she's a cool chick, and perfect for Rage. Obviously."

e

"Mm," I made the noise in the back of my throat, because it seemed to me that Rabbit had a bit of a crush on the woman, and that maybe his sage advice was also something he was trying to convince himself of. I knew there was no way Charlie had fucked him over, but maybe he wasn't as immune to catching feelings for people around the clubhouse as he pretended to be. Not that it mattered. We all had our fair share of secrets and reasons for doing the shit we did. I wasn't there to judge him any more than he was there to do the same to me.

"It goes both ways, you know?" I asked. He turned to look at me as he stood with his mostly empty plate in hand.

"What's that?"

"The offer to talk, if you ever need someone to listen."

Rabbit nodded and then cleaned up and headed out of the kitchen and the commons altogether.

"Hey, Tango!" Rage called out to me as he set his Old

Lady back down on her feet. "Need to talk to you about your room here at the clubhouse."

"I don't have one."

"There's one waiting, if you want to claim it." He tipped his chin up to someone else who came into the kitchen before turning his attention back to me. "Get with me later, and I'll sort it all out for you."

"Thanks," I agreed before cleaning up my own mess and hauling ass to go pack. Our lease on the apartment we were renting was damn near up, so this was perfect timing, since none of us wanted to rent the rat-trap for another year.

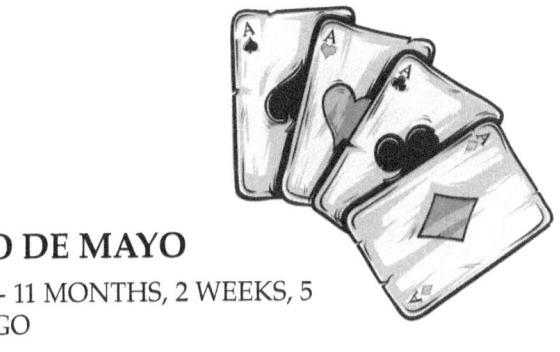

2. CINCO DE MAYO
TANGO - 11 MONTHS, 2 WEEKS, 5 DAYS AGO

FUCKING CINCO DE MAYO JUST WASN'T SOMETHING I REALLY wanted to get involved in. The holiday rankled in a way few people would understand, unless they knew my history with my ex-girlfriend, Camilla.

About a month before I got out of the military, Camilla asked me to attend a Cinco de Mayo party with her. We had been dating for two and a half years at that point. After coming home from a yearlong deployment, and expecting to propose to my girl, Cinco de Mayo seemed the perfect time to pop the question. We'd be around her family, friends, and fuck, I just couldn't wait to get a ring on her finger and officially take her off the market forever.

The minute I got to the apartment she shared with her two sisters, she grabbed my hand and pulled me upstairs to her bedroom. We fucked like crazy, with a condom, which I thought was odd, since we hadn't been using them before I went out on deployment. It was only after we fucked that she clued me in to why we were being so careful.

She'd met a boy from the neighborhood while I'd been gone. They were friends first, but soon fell in love, and with me not being there, apparently it had been easy for her to forget she was already involved with someone else. I guess all the Face Time videos, e-mails, and phone calls we had damn near daily when I wasn't down range hadn't mattered.

Not once had she mentioned the asshole. As if to add insult to injury, she then pulled a tiny little chip of a diamond ring out of her pocket and put it on the finger that I planned to slip my own ring on later that night. It was nothing like the ring that was burning up my pocket in that moment. She had gotten engaged to some other man while I was deployed.

I didn't say a word to her after she explained and slipped his ring back on her finger. I stood, walked out of her room, and left her apartment. I never looked back. I never answered a single text, call, or e-mail from her afterwards.

When her sisters begged me to take her back after she found out her fiancé, Pablo, was engaged to two other women in town, I ignored them. There was nothing to say, since their sister had cheated on me while I was off risking my fucking life for our country. To say that Camilla left me with trust issues was an understatement. I hadn't fucked a single woman since that night.

"Come on, man. I know all that shit went down on Cinco de Mayo two years ago, but it's time to build a new memory, maybe finally get laid again, dude." Whiskey told me as we pull up outside The Red Garter in Rapid City.

"Seriously, T, fucking use it or the thing's bound to fall the fuck off," Fox concurred. The bastard. He wasn't much better about women. Honestly, I sometimes wondered if he wasn't more into men, and afraid to admit it. Though, I don't know why he'd be afraid to admit it. It's not like any of us gave a fuck where he stuck his dick. None of my speculation mattered that night though, because my two best friends were on a mission to get me laid.

"Do you really think a strip club is the place to pick up chicks?" I asked incredulously. "Generally, the only women here are the ones working, and the hands-off policy in these places isn't going to get the job done." I smirked as I reminded them of that last little tidbit.

Whiskey's face fell into a thoughtful frown, but Fox laughed at me. "I have it on good authority there will be plenty of chicks here tonight. Some of the ladies from Black Hills Beauty College are here to cheer on a friend tonight."

"What the fuck, Fox? How the hell do you know that?"

He shrugged. "When I went on that run up here with Rabbit to chat with a distributor about the shit we needed over at Renegade Rosy's, we ran into a few of the girls. Shit man, we had a great time, and I've been texting with one of them on and off since."

Renegade Rosy's was the strip club the MC ran back in Spearfish, but seeing the same old tits and ass got old for some of us, which is why I thought we had come to Rapid City. At least, I thought that was why. The whole fucking night smelled like a setup with this new information.

"Well, shit!" I said while thinking back to the way I'd just been questioning Fox's sexuality. He was up front that he didn't mind a little fooling around with a dude, but I guess that's all there was to it, since he was actively seeking out this woman.

"What's her name, man?" Whiskey asked as something I couldn't really decipher flashed across his eyes before he locked it down.

"Mary," Fox announced before we paid our admission, and headed inside.

Fox had been right about the women being in abundance, but his Mary never did show up. Instead, a bubbly little redhead with a tight and toned body, slender hips, and a decent sized rack was all up in our business. She couldn't seem to decide between the three of us, which we all found amusing. We had shared a woman between us once before, when we were first picked up as full members of the club.

Most of my participation that night had come in the form of watching, and then getting my dick sucked. When I thought about that night and turned to see the redhead eyeing me up again while grinding on the dance floor between Whiskey and Fox, I thought maybe it would be the way to go again. I could get a blow job, ease some tension, and it would get my friends off my ass about fucking some random woman.

"So, are you guys hanging here all night, because Sadie just finished her last number, and the girls will be heading out soon?"

"You should definitely stick around with us, sweetheart," Whiskey informed her while giving a quick check that Fox and I were on board with that plan. We both nodded our agreement. Then he leaned in and used that smooth-as-fuck voice of his to send chills and goose bumps rolling across her skin. "You ever had three guys please you until you couldn't fucking move before?" Her eyes went wide, but not with shock. No, it was the anticipation of what was to come that had her pupils blown wide the wanting. The girl beside her, obviously a bit prudish, glared at her friend.

"Please, tell me you're not seriously going anywhere with these bikers," the girl snapped.

"I can't tell you that because I plan on going with them," the redhead laughed as she spoke to her friend.

"What about Jamie?" The girl asked.

"Well, if I hadn't caught Jamie fucking that cunt from Western Dakota, I'd pretend to be a nun whose legs had never been spread and leave with you." The guys and I laughed at her sassy response.

"Your man cheat on you, darlin'?" Fox asked. She batted her baby blues up at him and nodded. "Well, we'll make sure you forget all about him."

"Yes, please," she sighed. One of the other girls tugged on her arm then. "What?" The redhead asked. Her name still alluded me, not that it was important. She was nothing to me, and in the morning when we headed back to Spearfish, she'd still be nothing more than some girl who sucked me off while my two best friends fucked her in their own creative ways.

"Are you seriously going to hog all the sexy-as-fuck bikers?" This girl had blond bimbo written all over her. If she were auditioning to be a BRAT for the club, she'd probably stand a chance. As a one-night stand, who we had to be extra careful of, she didn't fit the bill. She stuck her tits out, though I wasn't sure why she wanted to make them look higher than they already were on her chest. Her mistake was aiming them my way. They were fake, not that I judged by that alone. The shape was nice, and their size was compatible with her stature, but there was no denying they were new to her since they sat so high and immovable on her chest.

If it weren't for the fact that everything else on her was just as fake as her tits, I wouldn't have minded. Unfortunately for the woman, her left eyelash was tilted at an odd angle where the glue hadn't held. her very dark roots were showing quite a bit, which had to be embarrassing for a beauty school attendee. Then there were her teeth which were all either capped with veneers, fake, or just bleached to high heaven. They were so white it almost hurt to look at them.

Dissecting the layers of makeup that she packed on would have been a full-time job. That was the thing that appealed to me most about the redhead. If she was wearing any makeup, it was minimal at best. She was rocking the natural look, and we were all down with that.

"What about you, handsome?" The blonde asked me. "You don't look like the type to share with two other men. I bet you could do all kinds of naughty things to me."

I grinned at her, probably giving her false hope, but the guys could tell by my grin that nothing good was about to come out of my mouth.

"Oh shit," Whiskey laughed before I even got a word out. I ignored him as my attention was caught once again by the woman's crooked fake eyelash.

"I could do lots of naughty things to you, sweetness," I told her while still grinning. She moved in closer, her breasts damn near molesting my arms. "But I would have to be interested in you, and I am most definitely not." Her eyes widened while her cheeks reddened in embarrassment.

"You see that girl there," I pointed to the redhead. "She's a natural beauty. I'd rather share someone like her with ten men than stick my dick in someone with eyelashes that look like a caterpillar is trying to make an escape from their face. Seriously, you should go get that shit in check."

"Holy fuck, Tango!" Fox sighed, shook his head, and then patted my arm as he doubled over in laughter. The redhead mouthed, "Thank you," to me even though it was unnecessary. It was not her fault that she could walk out of the bar with three virile, young guys ready to go throw down and her friends weren't any kind of competition. They could take their bitter jealousy and choke on it while my boys and I showed her a night she wouldn't soon forget.

I might even be convinced to get my dick wet for the first time in two years. The redhead should win an award for making that a possibility, considering the last two years had been a complete no-go where sex was concerned.

"Let's get out of here, beautiful." The redhead wrapped her arm around my bicep, and gladly accompanied me out of The Red Garter alongside my two best friends. We had checked into a hotel suite not far from there. Once we got to our bikes, I let go of the woman and helped her onto the back of Whiskey's bike for the ride over.

There had never been a woman on the back of my bike, and I wasn't about to make an exception for the stranger we picked up, even if she did get my dick hard. Whiskey didn't have the same beliefs about the back of his bike being sacred space for the woman who would be his old lady one day. He swore that he'd never have one to worry about.

"I can't believe that shit just rolled out of your mouth, man, but that was funny as fuck. I'm glad I wasn't the only one trying to figure out where her eyelashes were trying to run off to." Fox was still laughing, which was highly unlike him, so while I normally didn't take to insulting women, I was going to chalk it up as a win just because it got this reaction out of my friend. The bonus was that it also helped the redhead feel better about her decision to come with us.

BACK AT OUR HOTEL SUITE, we immediately cracked into the minibar since things got a little awkward after the ride. I'd only been in the one foursome before, and the only reason it hadn't been awkward that time was because we were all smashed, and the woman was a club whore. We didn't have to worry about how she'd feel about things in the morning. The same couldn't be said for the woman we'd just brought back to our hotel.

"Guys," Red finally called out as she knocked back a shot of rum. "This doesn't have to be weird." With that, she started stripping out of her clothes and both Whiskey and Fox followed suit almost immediately. She glanced at me, where I sat in a chair across from the action, taking it all in.

"What about you?" she asked, almost shyly.

"He likes to watch for a while first," Whiskey informed her as he slipped in behind her and reached around to grab her naturally abundant, creamy white tits that were capped with pale pink areolas and eraser-sized stiff nipples. My eyes tracked Fox as he strolled up in front of her, gliding his fingertips down her arms, just barely avoiding where Whiskey's arms overlapped as he mauled her breasts.

The two men watched each other for a moment, and the look that passed between them had sparks flying in the room that even my oblivious ass could sense. I hadn't been wrong before. There was more going on with my two best friends than what everyone saw on the surface. I wasn't so sure either of the morons realized they had a thing for the other, but it also wasn't my place to point that shit out. Maybe toying with this girl for a while would be enough to show them. Fox sank down to his knees in front of her and wasted no time leaning in and swiping his tongue through her sopping wet sex. I could see the dampness of her arousal trickling down her thighs from where I sat. Fox groaned as he took her in, obviously liking the taste of her. He wasn't one to fake that shit.

They played that game for a bit with Whiskey sucking at her neck, her jawline, the tops of her creamy mounds when he pushed them up with his large hands so that he could lean over her shoulder and suckle the tips while Fox continued to tickle her clit with his tongue. As I watched, my jeans grew tighter, so I unbuttoned, pulled the zipper down, and gripped my cock with my hand, giving it a bit of tug. Not that I needed it. I was rock hard just from the show the three of them were putting on.

Everything took place in slow-motion. That's how it felt as I ran my fist languidly up my shaft and back down again.

It was intoxicating, and completely different from the other experience the three of us had with the club whore. That experience had been about getting down to business and getting off as quickly as possible before we passed the fuck out. This was about exploration and enjoyment.

I really liked the fact that Red had a little landing strip of pubes leading from her tight belly to her sweet pussy that dripped with her own brand of honey that Fox couldn't seem to get enough of. Not many women kept any hair down there anymore, and what a shame that was, because it took away from the scent of a woman. Her arousal was easily whisked away with nothing there to capture it and entice a man to stick around. Hell, I'd never understand the desire of men to see a woman looking pre-pubescent anyway. Trimming was a good thing, since no one wanted to choke on pubes. A completely bald pussy just didn't do it for me though. I wanted my women to look like women.

I jerked out of my thoughts in time to see that Fox stood side by side with Whiskey while Red had each of her hands filled with their cocks. Neither of them was complaining about the change in position or her exploration. And while I'm not gay, or even bisexual, I will admit to being caught up enough that I was watching closely enough to notice that my best friends had very similar cocks. It was almost as if they were cut from the same cloth. Fox's was ever so slightly thicker than Whiskey near the head, but other than that they were about average length and girth for their build. They both knew how to use what they'd been given, too. Having witnessed it firsthand, there was no doubt.

Red kneeled before them and took turns licking first one,

then the other. She never took her hands off them as she did so. The hand that roamed up and down each of their shafts also dipped periodically to cup their balls and roll them around while she sucked deeply of each cock in turn. The guys were literally trembling in her hands as she worked. She moved to deep throat Fox, and he reached out, for the first time since she started worshipping at the altar of their cocks, to grab hold of her hair.

"Yeah baby, that's it. Suck it deep, because I'm about to blow." She followed directions well, sucking him in deep, hollowing out her cheeks, pulling hard, and rolling his balls around with her delicate hand.

"Fuck! Yeah!" Fox grunted as he shot his load straight down her throat. Little Red didn't stop there, though. No, she was a fucking champ, and made sure to lick him clean as she went.

Whiskey was all smiles as he moved closer to where I was sitting while Red licked Fox clean. I glanced over to see he had his cock in hand, giving it a firm pump as he took the seat beside me.

"C'mere babe. You need to take care of T like you just did Fox while I take care of that pretty pussy of yours." I could hear her moan as she stayed on her knees and crawled seductively over to where I sat, legs spread wide, and cock out at the ready. She gently removed my own hand from my cock and took its slightly longer, thicker flesh into her slender fingers.

Red didn't comment on my size like the BRAT back at the club had. I was thankful for that, even if the comparison hadn't bothered the other two men. Instead, she just went to work sucking, touching, and getting to know my cock and balls intimately. Whiskey had donned a rubber and moved in behind her sweet ass that wiggled in the air while she bobbed her hot, wet mouth on my dick. He ran two fingers up her slick folds eliciting a quick moan that reverberated through my cock in a beautiful way. The vibrations set me on edge as I threw my head back and willed myself not to blow just yet. It had been a while since I'd last indulged in a blow job. I wanted it to last, but the fact that it had been so long since I'd indulged was making it difficult.

After Whiskey impaled the woman with his dick, she cried out around my cock. I had to give her credit because she didn't let it stop her from treating my dick to a spectacular hand job before sliding me back into her hungry mouth.

Whiskey rocked in and out of her slowly, no doubt hitting her special spot each time as he did. I could tell because she would moan in delight at the same point with each push forward that he made. Her moans weren't what sent me tipping over the edge though. No, that happened the moment Fox moved up behind Whiskey, tapped his thighs apart further, and then lowered himself to his back, sliding beneath both Little Red and Whiskey to get at her clit with his mouth again. He sucked and licked her, and if I'm not mistaken, he enjoyed a fair bit of Whiskey as he pulled out each time too. Between Whiskey fucking her and Fox licking her, Red started panting and moaning a constant humming tune onto my dick as she sucked the life out of it. Literally. She sucked me until my balls pulled tight, lightning shot flashes of exquisite pleasure up my spine, and then thick, hot jets of my come shot into Red's mouth. She swallowed every last drop down while I relaxed back in pure fucking heaven. My head was thrown back on the chair as I waited for my limbs to start working again.

"Fuck, Red, you are so damn good at that." She chuckled at the compliment I paid her, but then her moans ticked up as Whiskey started pumping into her harder. I noticed Fox's hands were wrapped around Whiskey's thighs as he went to town on either one, the other, or both despite the pounding Whiskey was now giving the woman who was clearing shuddering under the weight of an intensely satisfying orgasm.

A moment after she tipped over, she took Whiskey with her. As he pulled out, the condom was shucked off by a separate set of hands, and he expelled the rest of his release into our friend's mouth. Red hadn't noticed that portion of the program, because she had collapsed face first onto my still denim-covered thighs.

As everyone came down from their respective orgasm induced highs, Red exploded in giggles.

"If this was supposed to be wrong, I don't think I ever want to be right again. Fucking fantastic!

I laughed and ran my fingers through her lovely hair. When I glanced up, the guys were watching what I was doing with an intensity that made me slightly uncomfortable. They'd been trying to 'fix me' since Camilla fucked me over. I wasn't sure that was possible, but there was something about the woman we'd picked up that I liked. Not necessarily in the respect that I would ever have a romantic relationship with her, but something screamed at me that we could at least be good friends. That was a step I hadn't even been willing to take with a woman in two years. So, it was progress in their eyes.

"You keep calling me Red,'" the woman said as she picked her head up off my thigh to look at me. I gave her a half-cocked grin but didn't respond. "Couldn't remember my name, huh?" She laughed, so I knew she wouldn't be offended by the truth.

I chuckled along with her. "Honestly, I don't remember you ever saying it, but I was lost in thought for a bit at the club."

"Lost in thought," she giggled. "Yeah, I bet that's what all the guys there were doing - getting lost in thought." She smiled brightly as I tucked her sweat-soaked hair behind her slightly pointy, elven-shaped ears. "I'm Amy, by the way. Amy Webber."

"Gavin Travers, but best to call me Tango or T, like these knuckleheads do," I offered. That was definitely far more than I'd offered any woman in far too long. Judging by the matching grins said knucklehead friends were throwing my way, I'd just done something to make them stupidly happy.

"Amy, when do you get out of school for the summer?" Whiskey asked.

"Two weeks, why?"

"How would you like to come hang out with us in Spearfish for a while?"

The grin on her face was answer enough. "I'd love to." That was the moment Amy Webber crash landed into the world of the Aces High MC, and our own personal, oddball little clique within the club.

3. GET OVER IT
TANGO - 11 MONTHS AGO

AMY WEBBER BREEZED INTO OUR WORLD AT THE CLUBHOUSE TWO weeks after we met her and quickly managed to charm everyone. The club members and regular hang-arounds couldn't figure out what was up with her though. When they saw the woman with Whiskey, Fox, or me it was obvious she was down for anything we wanted. She would flirt and be hands-on with any of the WTF crew. The first couple nights, it made some of the other men behave rather boldly with her, as if she was another BRAT we were bringing in. Confusion set in for those same men when Amy refused to flirt or respond in any way to their advances.

The first day Amy came to visit us, I joined in, and we had a replay of the night we'd all met her. It was an interesting time, and I got off in her hot little mouth again, but that's where it ended for me. I still wasn't ready to engage with another woman regularly for any purpose. Getting regular blow jobs and the thought of sex with one woman was out of the question, especially when that woman was already being shared between my two best friends.

"Hey, T!" Amy called out as I was eating my breakfast in the kitchen. I thought I'd had the place to myself, since most of the guys were partying pretty hard the night before, but I'd forgotten that the trio of Whiskey, Amy, and Fox had crashed a bit earlier than everyone else. Well, crashed probably wasn't the word, but they weren't drinking well into the hours of the morning.

"Amy," I acknowledged after swallowing the bite of food I'd just taken.

She glanced at me in an odd way, but then sat down across from me at the table and reached over to steal my toast.

"Are you upset with me?" Her eyes were clear, and didn't look accusatory, just curious.

"Nope, why would you think that?" I asked, giving her all my attention while I put my hungry stomach on hold.

"I just..." She hesitated a moment. "Well, you've only joined us the once since I've been here. The only reason I could think that you didn't join in anymore was that I'd somehow made you angry."

I smiled at her. "No, you haven't done anything. I'm not upset with anyone. The group shit is an occasional scene for me, not something I join in with on the regular. For the most part, I keep to myself."

"If you want it to just be the two of us one night, I'm sure the other guys wouldn't mind." The hopeful lilt of her voice set me on edge, but I hid my reaction well with a quick smile.

"That's not going to happen." It was an honest, if quick, explanation. I could tell by the frown on her face that it wouldn't be enough for her, so I fleshed out my answer a bit more. That wasn't something I'd normally do, but despite not wanting to have a relationship with any women, I didn't want to hurt her feelings.

"I don't mind joining in with you guys once in a while but being with a woman one-on-one isn't really in the cards for me right now."

She poked her lip out in a mock pout. "It's because your ex-girlfriend did a real number on you, huh?" she tossed out casually. I said nothing, narrowing my eyes slightly as she continued speaking. "The guys told me about what happened and said that you probably wouldn't be into doing much because of it."

Those mother fuckers. Amy was a nice girl, but we really didn't know her, and I didn't appreciate them sharing my history with her. I didn't even realize I had balled my fist up around my fork so tight that my knuckles were starting to turn white until a small, soft hand closed around them.

"I didn't mean to make you mad. I'm just trying to understand, and maybe help get you to move past what she did."

"I don't need a goddamn therapy session," I groused. "Whiskey and Fox need to keep their fucking mouths shut about shit that ain't there's to tell," I added as the two bastards in questions walked into the kitchen together. They stilled at my tone, and then glanced at Amy to make sure she was okay.

"You don't speak to her with that tone," Whiskey growled at me. My humorless laugh in response drew him up short.

"That last bit was meant for the two of you, not her, you big-mouthed motherfucker. My business is just that! Mine! Don't appreciate the two of you telling it to a stranger."

When Fox attempted to butt in, I narrowed my eyes further at him. "No! Just because you've fucked a few times doesn't make her anything more than a person you're fucking and getting to know. She doesn't get my past, my present, or my future unless I'm the one giving it. We clear?"

They both nodded while seeming contrite. I stood, pushed my plate away, and walked out of the room. There were times when it was best to get some space and some air.

AFTER WORK, I made my back to the clubhouse to find Amy sitting at the bar. There was no telling where Whiskey and Fox had run off to, but I made my way over to their new girl-toy to find out. Knowing Iceman, he wouldn't be too happy to find an unattended hanger-on sitting at the bar.

"Amy," I called to get her attention as I moved to stand beside where she was seated. Rabbit stood at the far end of the bar and tipped his chin up at me. The fact that he'd been watching her and waiting for someone to come collect the woman wasn't missed.

"Where are Whiskey and Fox?"

"Shower, I think." Her shoulders bobbed up and down

twice before she tipped her bottle of beer back to her lips. Then she took it away, lips still plump and pouty, as she tipped the beer bottle my way. "Want some?"

"Nah, I'm good."

"It wasn't my intention to piss you off earlier." It sounded almost like an apology, but there was a something missing from the way she spoke.

"Don't worry about it," I told her. My anger wasn't directed at you. It was meant for Whiskey and Fox."

"Because they told your secrets?"

"Because they shouldn't have told you anything about me to begin with, secrets or not."

"I see," she whispered before tipping her beer back up to her red-tinted lips. There was no denying the woman was beautiful. Her red hair was pulled up in some sort of loose, bun thing on her head with a few long curls that broke free to fall around her face. Her pretty blue eyes were rimmed in a gray liner that made the color of her irises pop. Her c-cup breasts were being hugged by a form-fitting gray sweater dress that was also doing amazing things for her ass despite her smaller stature and narrow hips. She knew how to play up the assets that worked best for her.

"You think you'll join us tonight?" she asked quietly.

I just shrugged my shoulders. "Guess it depends on how I feel later. Not exactly feeling the warm and fuzzies for the guys right now, so it might be awkward with me there."

"But you're never there for them anyway. They get off on being there together as much as they get off on me. I don't think that's the case with you."

"Well, I'm not going to tell you I don't enjoy watching,

because I do. It's like live porn that you get to join in on." I winked at her with my response to help make light of the statement I made.

She grinned. "Yeah, I guess it is that. Still, I think you're different."

"Maybe so, but I'm not the different that is going to come busting in and take you away from them for a one-on-one relationship, if that's what you're gunning for." The eye contact I made with her then was in an effort to drive my point home.

"That's good, because I don't want that. I think we all work well together, and you're all close, so it seemed like you three were a package deal from the start. I'm okay with that. I can't for the life of me explain why, because I've never done anything like it in my life, but when we're all together it just feels right. You know?"

I didn't respond beyond a quick nod of my head. I understood where she was coming from. It felt right to her. I wasn't about to judge, especially since I'd participated a couple times already, but I also knew it wasn't something I would be doing indefinitely. I wasn't ready for a real relationship with a woman again, but when the day came, it certainly wouldn't be with someone who wanted to share me with other men, even if those men were my two closest friends.

"When do you go back to school?" I finally asked, changing the subject.

"I see what you did there, but I'll let it go for now. I have two glorious months off before I need to go back. It'll be my last semester too. So, once winter rolls around, I will officially be licensed to cut and style everyone's hair." She laughed.

"Why the laughter?" I asked.

"Well, because it's obviously not an important job or anything." I wasn't sure who had made her believe that, but it wasn't something I could let go.

"Amy, every motherfucker here needs a trim from time-to-time. Imagine what we'd look like if we attempted to do it ourselves." I cringed in mock horror. "Then there's the old ladies, BRATs, and dancers we have who all need their hair cut, styled, colored, permed, or whatever else they're doing to hair these days. Someone has to do it. Your job is important. Don't ever let anyone demean you for it. So, you're not a doctor! Guess what? You won't have the stress of possibly screwing up and killing someone daily. You will earn a paycheck, and its legitimate money. You should be proud of that."

The brilliant smile that bloomed on her face told me that she needed to hear someone validating her career choice. "Thank you for that!" she finally told me while still grinning like she'd just won a prize.

"I am here to boost your ego anytime you need it!" I joked with her when Whiskey finally made his way to us.

"What's going on? We walked into the bar and saw you lighting up like fireworks on the Fourth of July?" Whiskey asked her as he wrapped the woman in his arms.

"Nothing much. T was just telling me I should be proud of my schooling and my future career."

"Well, yeah, you should. Speaking of that," he started when Fox walked up. "We were talking to Mila from Rosy's earlier and she said that Janice is going to be moving on soon, since her boyfriend is joining the Marines. She's the one that does hair for all the girls over there. I was thinking, with the timing being what it is, you might be able to slide right into that position once Janice leaves. It'll help the girls out of a bind and get you that first paying gig until you can find something or set up your own place like you were talking about."

"I'm glad I made it here before you spilled the beans without me, asshole!" Fox joked while punching Whiskey lightly on the bicep. "What do you think of that?" he turned to ask my opinion.

"I think it's a great idea. Everyone loves you," I offered, turning to Amy. "You don't mind dealing with bikers or the women that are around, so that makes you damn near perfect for the job, really."

Amy squealed then, as if she'd been waiting for my approval, too before getting excited. "Really?" She finally squeaked as she looked at each of us in turn. "Oh my God, I'm so excited! I can't believe how lucky I am!"

Three Weeks Later

"CAN I ASK YOU A QUESTION?" Amy inquired as she threw her arms around my neck, hugging me from behind as I sat in the kitchen chair trying to have my morning coffee.

"Of course," I answered and waited for her to come

around to face me for the conversation. Instead, she leaned in over my shoulder and placed a kiss at the corner of my mouth before moving her lips closer to my ear and speaking. "Why haven't you come to bed with us lately?"

It had been a week since I'd participated in their little sexcapades. Truthfully, I wasn't exactly interested, but kept bowing down to pressure from either Whiskey or Fox to be a part of their endeavors. Part of me did it just to prove I was okay, because I knew that's what they were looking for when they invited me. Still, that didn't make answering the question much fun.

"I'm not oversexed like the rest of you," I started to explain when I felt her tense up behind me. "Look, it's nothing personal, and I'm not judging anyone. I just, I don't need or want it like the others do." I shrugged and tried to blow it off, but that was when Amy moved to sit on my lap with her arms still draped around my neck.

"I get differences in sex drives, but is that the only thing keeping you away, or is there something more I can do?" She pouted, as if that would make me give into what she wanted. The problem was, I hated that manipulative shit. Amy got insecure every few days or so if I continued to turn down a romp with everyone. It had become such a fucking problem that I had asked Iceman, our club president, to consider me for the next out of town run. I didn't care what it was. I just needed to be gone for a while. I already caught enough shit from Whiskey and Fox. The last thing I needed was pressure from their girlfriend, too.

"I already told you, all of you, that it's not like that. I'm busy trying to open my shop. It's exhausting." I was about to add to the sentiment that I just wasn't that into it when one of the BRATs walked in, saw Amy on my lap, and hissed in her general direction.

"How many of the boys are you going to try to fuck at once, Amy? You do know you only have three holes, right?" Amy stiffened in my arms.

"You better mind yourself," I called out to the woman, whose name I couldn't have remembered if my life depended on it.

"I don't get it," she continued, as if I hadn't just given her a warning. "Does she have a magic fucking pussy or something? I mean she's got the entire W.T.F. brood all hemmed up in her shit. There must be something special," the woman spat out snidely. It was the first time someone had mentioned me as a part of their little sex-group in my presence and I wasn't certain how I felt about the inclusion. Sure, I joined in with them occasionally, but no one really knew that I never had sex with her. Hell, I never even worked at pleasing her, if I was being honest. I just took my visuals, my blow job, and went about my business. I let the other two take care of her needs, because again, and I hated to sound like an asshole, but they kept inviting me, and it didn't matter to me if I was there or not.

The sweet butt carried on with her anti-Amy tirade, though. "Maybe, your pussy is just so loose that you need more than one dick in a hole to feel full."

Amy stood and turned to face the nasty little bitch that spewed filth about her. "You earn your place here by sucking anyone's dick who asks. Your holes are open to any of the brothers, their hangers-on, and visiting members. I'm not judging, but you sound a lot like the pot who called the kettle black. Except we're not the same. I have my own place to live, my own money to spend, and I'm here only because I want to be. I'm here because I'm having fun with *MY* boys, not because they pay me to be a toy. I only have sex with *MY* boys. They don't share me with anyone who pops through the front door. I'm sorry that you're jealous, but that's your problem."

"They're not *YOUR* boys, sweetheart!" The club whore spat back at her. Then her evil grin should have been a clue as to what was coming next, but I didn't catch on until it was too late. "Sherry-Baby had all three of them together before you ever came along. What you got ain't some special thing for them. You're just the next three-hole toy for them to fuck together."

Amy couldn't hid the hurt that traced across her face momentarily before she schooled her features and responded. "Then I'm sure Sherry-baby knows why I choose to have my fun with them!" Amy started to walk off, and I got up to follow her. Before I left, I turned back to the whore.

"Be warned, I'm putting you on notice now, you get in Amy's face again, and I will put you out on your ass with or without the club's approval. She's not a disposable whore, but you can be replaced like that," I snapped my fingers together to show just how quickly it could happen. The woman gasped and sputtered but didn't dare say a word back to me. They all knew better than to talk back to a brother who was putting them in their place. Once I finished, I took off after Amy to make sure she was okay.

"Amy," I called out, and took a couple steps to catch up to

her before pulling her over into a little alcove created by a bay window that faced the courtyard out back. "Listen to me, before you go thinking things that aren't true. The boys and I were only with one woman together before you, and that was the night we were inducted as full members here. We were so fucked after all the shots they made us down that night that none of us even knew which sweet butt it was that we shared. I had no clue it was Sherry-Baby. To be honest, I still couldn't tell you which one that is without getting someone to point her out."

Amy cringed, and I laughed. "Yeah, I feel about the same. It wasn't one of my finest moments, and all of us were tested afterward just to be sure. There was evidence someone used condoms, but honestly, none of us could remember much beyond walking into a room together and waking up in a tangle of body parts and being completely hung the fuck over. You were a decision we all made that first night, without alcohol weighing us down and making us forget where we were and who was keeping us company."

"I get it. No need to placate me. I figured you guys all had a history before I came into the picture. It was tough to hear it from her, considering the shit she was saying, but I'm not upset with you or the guys." Amy's sweet disposition wasn't a surprise. Despite her kinky proclivities in the bedroom, she really was one of the most positive women I'd known in a long while.

I leaned down and kissed her forehead. "I have to go get shit ready for a late-night client. Let's make sure the guys know about that cunt, and to watch your back for you before I head out, okay?"

Amy smiled and nodded at me as I grabbed hold of her hand and pulled her along to find Whiskey and Fox. She might not have been my girl, but she had become a good friend, and I had no doubt that Whiskey and Fox were planning to keep her around. That meant I would do whatever was necessary to keep her protected.

4. THEIR SCENE
TANGO - 4 MONTHS, 5 DAYS AGO

I PICKED AMY UP AND SPUN HER AROUND IN A CIRCLE CAUSING HER cap to go flying. Whiskey chased after it while Fox laughed at the spectacle.

"So proud of you, Amy!" I squeezed her into a tight hug as if to prove my point. She had gone back to school after spending the summer at the clubhouse. She still visited most weekends but had to stay in Rapid City during the week. When she didn't come down, Whiskey and Fox usually went to her, unless we had a work obligation. I opened Liquid Lines in September, and my busiest days were on the weekends, so I never did find the time to get away to go see her during the times when she couldn't come to the clubhouse.

Amy's graduation meant that she would be moving to Spearfish permanently. The girls from Renegade Rosy's had convinced Janice to stay on until Amy could graduate. Whiskey and Fox extended the invitation for her to live at the clubhouse with them until she could find a place of her own in town. I assumed the guys would end up spending more time with Amy once she did move into her own place, but that was still up in the air. I didn't really care, so long as all my friends were happy.

I put Amy down, transferring her to Fox who had been impatiently waiting for me to finish manhandling her so that he could do so. Amy seemed a bit put off by the fact that I only kissed her forehead as I released her to my friend. Maintaining my distance from her had been imperative since I'd been getting certain vibes from her recently. There might not have been a woman in my life for a few years, but I still knew what it meant when they got that determined look in their eyes. I was honestly happy for Amy and proud of the fact that she'd just graduated, but I should have curbed my enthusiasm when celebrating with her.

Fox gave me a bit of a squirrelly look as he pulled his girlfriend into his arms and swung her around before planting a heated kiss on her lips right there for everyone to see. There were people openly gawking, considering she'd just been manhandled by another biker with a third eyeing the woman hungrily as he approached.

"My turn!" Whiskey called out as he snatched a giggling Amy from Fox's arms and planted a not-safe-for-public-consumption style kiss on her lips as well. To say some of the families in attendance were scandalized would be an understatement.

"We better get out of here, guys. Looks like we're attracting the wrong kinds of attention," I nodded to the campus cops that were meandering in our general direction. Honestly, they appeared to be taking their time about it while stopping to cajole people who were making complaints instead of letting them get to us in a timely manner. We all four turned and headed to the van we borrowed from the club for the day. We had loaded all of Amy's things in it earlier, before the ceremony, so that we could hit the road immediately afterward.

"We have something special planned when we get home," Fox told her when she inquired as to why we weren't going out to dinner first before heading back to Spearfish. The club was putting on a hell of party in Amy's honor. It was going to be a graduation-slash-new employee-slash-welcome to the family type thing. Neither Whiskey or Fox had claimed her yet, but everyone figured it was coming soon.

When we got there the lights were already low, the music turned up, and it was clear most of our brothers and their women had started the party without us. That was just fine by me. I wanted to celebrate with the guys and Amy, but I was also dog-ass tired from putting so many hours into my new tattoo studio. I had the club's backing on it, but Iceman was gracious enough to let me take control and run with my ideas. Being the man I am, a perfectionist at heart, I took everything seriously and ended up doing most of the work myself.

Amy was whisked away to the bar immediately, by Whiskey and Fox, to get her caught up on the celebration.

"How come you're not over there getting your girl trashed too?" I turned to see the club's Vice President, Rage, eyeing me quizzically.

I tipped my head in the direction of the threesome, who were laughing about something while doing shots. "Her boys have her handled." Rage's brow tipped again in question, but I simply shrugged my shoulders. What was I going to say? I joined them once in a while when they pestered me to the point where I just need to shut them the hell up. Amy was a friend, but she was definitely not my girl. I haven't needed a steady girl in my life since Camilla fucked me over. I sure as fuck wasn't going to share the first woman who I made a commitment of any kind to. If I was going to do that, I could have stayed with my cheating ex-girlfriend.

Thankfully, I didn't have to explain myself, or the awkward situation my buddies kept putting me in, any further. Charlie, Rage's old lady, wandered up and stole his attention away from me with a heated kiss that caused a few hackles to raise amongst the BRATs of the clubhouse. They had all been salivating over the club's VP long before Charlie showed up. To her credit, Rage's old lady didn't take any of their shit and had already managed to have a few of them ousted from the clubhouse because of their behavior. I admired her for that. The woman didn't put up with a hell of a lot from anyone, least of all our scary ass VP even though most sane people wouldn't stand toe-to-toe with him.

"Hey there Tango," Charlie finally acknowledged me after reluctantly pulling away from her man's mouth.

I grinned at her. "Don't let me interrupt your warm hello to Rage."

She laughed at me before turning her attention to the bar as well. "Shouldn't you be over there getting in on that action, too?"

I glanced toward the bar to see that both Whiskey and Fox had Amy sandwiched between them, each devouring a different part of her with their mouths. Whiskey was sucking on her neck. The only thing keeping the rest of the room from seeing her pretty, pale nipples was the fact that Fox had one sucked into his mouth and the other covered with one of his hands. I crinkled my nose in disgust. I wasn't judging them, but if she was my girl, her tits wouldn't be on display for everyone else to see. Charlie and Rage both gave me an odd look before I managed to school my features.

"Nope, that's their scene," I stated.

"Oh, I thought…" Charlie's voice trailed off as Rage pulled her in a bit tighter to his body and whispered something in her ear.

"I'm gonna head on over and play a round." I pointed in the direction of the pool tables while the couple just offered me a placating smile. Who knew what they were thinking. Probably thought there was some jealous bullshit going down, but honestly, I was just getting frustrated with always being associated with that crap. To each their own. I loved my friends and supported their choices. Their choices just didn't line up with the way I wanted to live my life on the regular.

Rabbit had a woman bent over backwards on the pool table and was basically dry humping her there when he shot me an evil grin. "You wanna play too?"

"Yeah, pool, motherfucker, how 'bout you move her ass so I can get to it?" I knew I sounded grumpy, but I'd gone from being happy for Amy and her graduation to just being tired as fuck of having that whole scenario shoved off on me like it was a forgone conclusion.

"Get on out of here," Rabbit told the woman as he pulled

her lithe frame off the furniture and smacked her ass to send her on her way. I didn't know why he bothered to pretend. The man wasn't one to play around with the club girls, at least not that I'd ever seen. Considering I was in sour mood because I hated that people were painting me with the same brush they did Whiskey and Fox, I guessed it would be best not to make further assumptions about Rabbit's proclivities or lack thereof.

"Rabbit," the woman whined, which made him bristle.

"Club business, now get gone!" he commanded her, and that time without the playfulness he showed previously. She snapped to attention and left us to it as Rabbit grabbed the balls and started racking them. "So, what's eating you?"

I shrugged my shoulders while chalking my cue.

"Have anything to do with the show your boys are putting on over there?"

I laughed, not even having to look behind me to see that things are probably getting a bit out of control. Amy would have zero regrets about all the public displays tomorrow. The guys wouldn't have any either. If I had been involved, the same wouldn't be able to be said. "Not in the way you might think."

Rabbit's smirk faded. "Not into sharing, huh?"

"Not particularly."

"Is that a problem for you, or just not your scene?" he asked the question, legitimately concerned that I might be jealous, or take issue with my boys.

"Not my scene in any respect, man."

"Why go there at all then?"

I huffed out a sigh before I took the shot sending the balls scattering as two solids slid into opposite corners.

"Nice shot," Rabbit conceded, and then waited for me to answer.

"Sometimes, it's just easier to use the situation to take the edge off. Other times, it's a fuckin' headache to be associated with that shit."

"So, she belongs to Whiskey and Fox, but not you?"

"She belongs only to them only, if that's how they see her. I don't want to speak for them either, since they haven't officially claimed Amy yet."

Rabbit nodded his head as though I'd just admitted something he was already aware of. I didn't take him for the observant type, since he was the consummate joker in the club, but the shrewd look behind his eyes clued me in. He had already known where I stood with the trio and was simply clarifying so I could blow off steam.

"Does it bother you that people associate you with all that?" He swirled his cue around indicating whatever was taking place behind me still.

"Nah, their assumptions are based on what they think they see, I get it. I'm hoping that the three of them get on board with me not being a part of it, though ."

"Lucky for you, even if she's a clinger, she has two other dicks to fall on, huh?"

I laughed at that, grabbed the beer that Shameless handed me as he sauntered over, and took a good long pull from it. "Let's hope," I stated when I come up for a breath. Shameless shook his shaggy head back and forth, grinning at me, having obviously heard enough to get the gist of what Rabbit's statement was about.

"Bunch of men 'round here would kill to have your problems," he joked.

"Well, from what I understand, my problems are on full display over there. They're welcome to 'em." The three of us laughed off the rest of the night as I schooled Rabbit in the fine art of using a pool table for its actual intended purpose. To play the game instead of running game, or a train, or whatever else he pretended he was going to do with that woman earlier.

I ended up crashing in the room I had at the clubhouse that night. Being trashed, thanks to Shameless and Rabbit constantly throwing another drink in my hand made it impossible for me to do anything else. Besides that, the only place I had to go was to the little three-bedroom house the guys had rented with the hopes that Amy would move in with them once she was settled in her new job.

I wasn't sure if Amy knew about that yet, since she thought the plan was for her to stay at the clubhouse with them until she found a place. I figured it was going to be a graduation surprise, after the surprise party the club threw for her.

5. CLAIMING THE GIRL
TANGO - 3 WEEKS, 4 DAYS AGO

WHISKEY AND FOX HAD BEEN SHACKED UP WITH AMY FOR A FEW months while I continued to stay at the clubhouse. They continued to try to get me to move into the house they'd rented. There were three rooms, four people. I did the math, and it didn't work in my favor. They swore that the three of them were usually situated in the master bedroom together anyway, so there was plenty of room.

I refused and managed with my room at the clubhouse just fine. There were nights the three of them would invite me to join them, and once in a while when they were staying at the clubhouse for the night, I took them up on the offer. I wasn't proud of the fact, and usually felt ashamed of myself the following day.

It wasn't the group sex that bothered me. I was ashamed because of my reasons for going there to begin with. Mostly, I was tired of hearing them complain about how all I ever did was work and never went out to find a woman to take the edge off. The other reason was that I needed to take the edge off and I thought getting blown by Amy, while my friends were in the middle of their usual shenanigans, would be more drama free than some of the other clingy women in the clubhouse.

I continued to avoid the inevitable discussions with my best friends, and Amy herself, about me moving in the house with them. I knew why they continued to harass me about it and that's exactly why avoided talk of becoming the fourth person in their household. I already felt enough pressure to join in with them on the nights they partied at the clubhouse. Hell, I'd come to my room a time or two to find them all crashed out there waiting on me. Those were the nights I had to fight myself to stop an angry outburst, because I didn't want my personal space invaded by anyone else, not even my own best friends. Sometimes, I would turn around and go back to sleep on a couch in my shop so that I wouldn't blow a fucking gasket and ruin our friendship.

It didn't help the situation that I would come back the next day to see Amy roaming around the clubhouse wearing one of my shirts, like I'd given it to her. I knew I'd have to get it through their heads eventually that I wasn't interested in being an invested member of their scenario, but up until then, I'd taken the path of least resistance in order to keep the peace.

My peace was fading fast though.

"You gonna be a grump again tonight, or are you going to join in for some fun?" Her voice, being made purposely sultry the way it was, grated on my nerves as she came up and put a hand on my back possessively. When I didn't respond immediately, she dug her nails in just enough to make it known she was there and wanted my undivided attention.

I grunted a half-assed response to her that I couldn't even understand myself.

"Ah, grumpy then?" she questioned on a playful laugh.

I continued working on the sketch I was doing for a client. I was bent over the bar and focused on the details. That meant, I didn't want to be disturbed. Inspiration came and went far too easily, and distractions were unwelcome as a result. I wanted to drink my coffee and finish the project before I lost interest again and had to put it up for another day.

Amy didn't take the hint though. Instead, she trailed her fingers up my back lazily, as if she had every right to touch me in such an intimate way. Her fingers stopped where my hairline started at the nape of my neck where I keep it trimmed close, as opposed to the longer, inky black spikes I wore on the top.

"I just want you to be as happy as the rest of us," she purred.

I stopped what I was doing and turned an aggravated glare up at her. "Who says I'm not happy?"

"If you were happy, you'd smile more and join us. Last night, when we celebrated the guys asking me to be their old lady, you should have been there too. You ended up no-showing on us again."

"That was your celebration with Whiskey and Fox," I explained to her. "I'm not sure why you couldn't have it at your own place." The previous night had been another one where I found them all having another fuck-fest in my club room. Just the thought made me straighten my back up to pop my spine in an attempt to knock the kinks out of it. The couch in my studio was comfortable, but it was still lacking what my slightly achy body needed. Once I felt the instant relief that stretch brought on, I turned my attention back to Amy who had finally removed her hand and was offering up another one of her infamous, pouty looks.

I didn't bother pandering to the pout that time. I honestly didn't give a fuck why in the hell she was upset, and I was tired of playing therapist to Whiskey and Fox's old lady.

"Look, I need to get this done for my client. He's coming by later to check it out and approve it before we get to work on his back piece."

Amy stared at me a moment before her whole upper body seemed to crumple in on itself. Nope. I wasn't going to feel bad this time. She wasn't mine to entertain, and if she made the other guys feel that way all the time, I could see why it took more than one of them to be in a relationship with her. She was non-stop work in the moments where the party stopped, and everyone had to live their real, adult lives. Lately, she had started feeling a whole lot more like work I didn't need to do and a lot less like the good-time Amy of old who I managed to be friends with.

Amy turned on her heel in a huff and sauntered off, shaking her hips like I'd seen many of the club girls do over the years. I shook off the encounter and continued working on the back piece that had been the bane of my existence for the last couple days.

"You need anything, Sugar?" Cherry asked. She normally

worked over at Renegade Rosy's, but I'd seen her more and more at the clubhouse, usually whenever Rabbit's brother, Spinner, was around.

"Nah, I'm good."

"Okay, well I'm working the bar today since Charlie had somewhere to be. If you need anything, just yell, otherwise I won't bother you, since you look busy."

"I appreciate that, Cherry."

"How do you always know it's me, and not my sister?"

I smiled up at her then. "You're far nicer than your sister."

Cherry laughed. "Well, that's the truth and a half." She continued chuckling as she walked away and moved toward where the other guys who were hanging around were congregated at the opposite end of the bar.

"You ready for tonight?" The question was issued as Iceman sat to my right nearly twenty minutes later. I moved to put my sketch away along with all my other crap I'd inadvertently spread over the top of the bar in front of me.

"This isn't for tonight," I explained. "I have a client coming in, but he texted and put it off until tomorrow."

Iceman grinned at me. "I wasn't talking about the ink, but that's a mighty fine piece you'll be doing from the looks of it."

"Yeah, it is. I imagine it'll have to be done in a couple sittings at least. Judging by the amount of color work and detail, I'm looking at a good ten hours of work, minimum."

Iceman nodded at my assessment. "Imagine so," he agreed.

"What did you mean, am I ready for tonight?"

His eyebrows pinched together as if he were thinking hard, then he glanced around. Not seeing what he was looking for, he turned back to me. "You know, with the little patching ceremony the guys are throwing together for Amy?"

It was my turn to question him once again. "Not following."

Iceman stared at me a moment a longer, and then he grinned. "Fuck's sake, you know it's not a secret from me, since they had to get approval, but if that's how you want to play it fine." He snagged a beer from Cherry. "I'll be in my office for a bit. Have some last-minute shit to tidy up before I join the party tonight. Finally got Carol out of here, so I might actually be able to have a good time."

Carol was Iceman's estranged wife and disgraced old lady. She'd shown her ass one too many times around the club to be allowed back around, and when she was banned from coming to the clubhouse for a short time, she threw an outrageous fit and made things far worse for herself.

Last I heard, Iceman had filed for divorce, and put out a club-wide mandate that Carol wasn't allowed near the club in any capacity. She had a son that was now with the Sierra High Chapter in Georgia, but apparently, she wasn't welcome there either. I still had no clue what Iceman had been inferring earlier, but I assumed some sort of party would be happening tonight, so I finished packing my shit up and took it all up to my room on the second floor.

When I got up to my room, there was a note lying on my bed, which reminded me that I apparently needed to start locking my damn door. I picked up the note to read the demand in whiskey's nearly illegible scrawl that my presence was required tonight, and that 'No' was not an answer. Fine. Tonight, I was going to put all three of my friends in their place and tell them I wanted nothing else to do with their extracurricular activities.

I'd had a shit day, so I went to lie down and get a fuckin' nap in, especially since my presence was requested at another party that night. When I woke, it was to the sound and vibration of loud music, and even louder assholes. Apparently, I had slept through part of the party after all.

By the time I got downstairs, the music screeched to a halt as my buddies climbed up on the stage the strippers usually used. They dragged Amy up on the stage with them. I guessed this was going to be their formal announcement that they'd claimed her.

"You all know Amy's our girl, been that way a while," Whiskey started out in his usual jovial tone. Weird that he had a 'usual' jovial tone these days, since he was once the grumpier of the three of us.

"Tonight, we officially claim this gorgeous woman as ours," Fox finished for our brother as he held out a smaller version of the leather kutte they both wore. Only, when they turned her around, after putting it on her, the top rocker read, 'Property of W + F,' which caused everyone to start yelling like the lunatics they were.

"Don't think I've ever seen a woman claimed by more than one man of the club before. This is new," Shameless said to me as we both snagged a beer from Charlie who beamed at us from the other side of the bar.

"I don't doubt that. I'm waiting to see how it plays out long term myself," I admitted.

Shameless grinned at me while giving an odd sidelong glance. "Why aren't you up there celebrating with them?"

I waved off his question. "This is their moment, let them have it. No need to put my ass in the middle of their business."

Shameless, once again, tossed an odd look my way before glancing back at Charlie. I caught him shrugging his shoulders at her while she just continued to smile. I felt like the idiot who didn't know he was the butt of some joke everyone else was in on. I didn't get long to think on it, since Whiskey plopped a squealing Amy into my lap before I could stop him.

"What the hell?" I asked as Amy smiled sweetly at me while trying to clamp her hands around the back of my neck.

Fox clapped his hand down on my shoulder, distracting me from her proprietary move. "Where were you, man? We had to start without you, so that kinda sucked."

"I saw everything," I explained quickly. All three of them stilled and stared at me. Once again, I was left to feel like the asshole on the wrong side of a joke. I was too fucking tired to care. My recent nap aside, I had been feeling exhausted lately. "Look, I'm spent. I've been pulling long hours with shop and getting ready for the Reno trip coming up." They all got that look like I'd just kicked their cat or something. "Congrats on all this," I stated while depositing Amy onto her feet in front of Whiskey. "Seriously, I'm happy for the three of you."

"Happy for us?" Amy asked with a cautious tone.

"Yeah," I agreed, giving the hair on her head a playful little toss. "Happy for all of you. I promise, I'll take you guys out to celebrate your claim on one another soon. I just need to crash tonight." I didn't wait for them to say anything, talk me out of leaving the part, or invite themselves back to my room. For the first time since I joined the club, I locked my door to bar anyone from getting in. A little later, I listened as the doorknob jiggled followed by my friend's incredulous outburst beyond my door wondering what the hell was wrong with me.

They wanted to know what was wrong with me, but the answer wasn't something they would like. Worse, it was something that I'd been struggling with. I was beginning to resent my two best friends for continually putting me into a position I didn't much care to be in. Their need to feel like they 'fixe me' was about to break me instead. I just had to find a way to get them to understand that not wanting to be a part of their group shit didn't have anything to do with still being hung up on, or running from, the issues Camilla left me with. It had everything to do with the fact that I didn't want to be a part of that lifestyle. I'd been supportive of them and the fact that they couldn't offer me the same support was getting old quick.

I was headed to Reno soon for the Lady Luck Tattoo Arts Expo. I was hoping that by the time I got back things would be a bit more settled for the three of them. Then, maybe I wouldn't be walking right back into the same old drama, because I was damn near at my breaking point where feelings were going to get hurt, and friends might be lost.

6. LADY LUCK LISTENS
LIZA - 2 WEEKS, 6 DAYS AGO

My brother was going to die. I couldn't believe he had put me in a position where I was in this much danger. Actually, I could, because this wasn't the first time, and I had the scars to prove it. Why, oh why, did I continue to love my brother?

I stood off to the side of the booth the stranger in front of me had set up. He hadn't yet noticed me, and my brother didn't give a shit if I overheard them or not, since I already knew the score.

"I really appreciate you taking on my sister like this. I owe you and the club, big time."

"You know they're not entirely happy with me agreeing to get involved considering you dug this hole you're in all by yourself," the man stated. Truthfully, I respected the hell out of him for saying that. At least I knew he wasn't being bowled over by my big brother with a bunch of lies and the same happy horseshit he fed everyone else.

I took another, harder look at the man in question. He was the person I was supposed to be leaving my life here in

Reno with. I was to ride out with him when the expo was over and then stay hidden in the black hills of South Dakota. Being stuck in the middle of no-fucking-where didn't exactly thrill me. Cold weather and whatever they had going on up there was not my scene. Then again, I supposed anything was better than being hunted, raped, and tortured by my brother's enemies.

I'd avoided the rape part last time he was in trouble, but only just so. Some days, I still can't believe I ever forgave him, and allowed the rat-bastard back into my life. I thought he had changed. Finding out I was wrong meant that my life was being turned upside down.

"I know. I know. I can't," my brother actually choked up. "Last time," he tried again, and had to collect himself. "They did things to her once before, man. I couldn't live with myself if anything ever happened to her again. I fucked up, but I didn't realize who he was when I stole his girl. I swear, I don't owe money, I'm not involved in drugs or any other shady shit. I fucked the wrong girl. I know what they'll do, though. They'll go after my sister, because she's important to me."

The other man shook his head at my brother. "I don't even know what to say about that shit. You're sure that's all that went down?" he asked, and it didn't seem like the first time. The man must have been at least a little smart to question my brother's story. I was having a hard time believing it, too. The only reason I gave him the benefit of the doubt was because I got to meet Michelle.

She swore that Random, her ex-boyfriend and the VP of the King's Demons MC, was beating her and she had run from him before she met my brother. I believed their story, because there was no way my brother's new girlfriend could fake the fear and worry that I saw in her eyes. I wanted them protected, because Michelle was now pregnant with my niece or nephew, but I also wanted to know why my life was the one being disrupted and not theirs.

"Why do you think they're coming for your sister, and not this woman you knocked up?"

"Michelle. He doesn't want her anymore, because she has another man's baby in her belly. She's considered 'tainted' now. They've taken Liza before and didn't get to finish what they started with her. He's already made threats about doing just that." My brother made a noise that sounded entirely too much like the low warning growl an animal might make.

"I can't let them do that to her. She's a good girl. Well, she ain't a saint," he offered with a chuckle. "My sister has a foul-as-fuck mouth, but a great heart. You know? It's fucked that I have to lose her talent too."

"Seriously? You're worried about not having her around because she's an artist, not because you put a fucking bullseye on your sister's back?" The man asked incredulously.

"You know what I mean," my brother huffed. "I love my sister. I'm going to miss her for a lot of reasons."

"Where is this sister of yours?" The man asked. His broad shoulders and short cropped black hair that spiked up on top were pretty much all I had been able to see of him. That and the fact that his ass filled out his jeans in a wonderful way, and his left arm appeared to be sparsely inked from the elbow down, which I found interesting for a tattoo artist. He towered over my brother's five feet, eleven inches of height, so I almost missed it when my brother pointed in my direction. The man turned and I was immediately captivated by his unusual eye color. It appeared to be an odd blend of green and gold that would look amazing as cat eyes, but his were a bit too rounded to be considered feline. It worked for him though. The man was hotness personified. The front view rivaled the backside I'd been staring at throughout their conversation.

"C'mere, Liza!" My brother called out, forcing me to step forward and acknowledge the two men who I had been eavesdropping on. I move forward, stepping around the barricade that blocked pedestrian traffic into the man's booth space.

"This is my sister," Frankie explained. "Liza Rossi," he offered while gesturing between the stranger and myself. "Sis, this is Tango with the Aces High MC." I had noticed the MC kutte sitting on a chair off to the side. He wasn't supposed to wear it in the booths, as per the rules, but that didn't mean he was going to let it get too far from his person either.

I glanced back over my shoulder at my brother's deep-set brown eyes that smiled down at me reassuringly. "Are you sure about this? He's with a motorcycle club," I stated plainly. "As in the same kind of people who are after me."

"He's with the good kind, Sis. I promise, I wouldn't send you with anyone who would even think of laying an unwanted hand on a woman." The man stayed quiet while watching me with those intense eyes of his. The damn things were even more spectacular up close.

I turned and stuck my hand out to shake Tango's. He gripped mine with a large, warm hand that sent zinging energy right up my arms and caused me to break out in a serious case of goose bumps. I glanced up into a chiseled face that was shadowed by the black stubble that grew along his jaws and cheeks. Even though it was noticeable, the hairs there were still very short, as if he had simply forgotten to shave for a day or two instead of being a purposeful look.

"Good to meet you." He released my hand before directing his attention back to my brother. "I'll be finishing out the weekend here before we head out. Is that going to be a problem?"

"I don't think so. Is it possible for her to work here as your assistant instead of in my booth for the duration though? I figure the sooner we establish distance, the better."

I turned a sharp glare on my brother. The asshole was acting as though we were still living 200 years ago and he was trading me off for a goat, two chickens, and a pig with the way he was negotiating my custody turnover. I damn near called off his insane plan until I caught sight of a kutte in the crowd that clearly had a King's Demons patch on it.

"Frankie?" I called to him, and tipped my head in that direction.

"Fuck! I didn't think any of them would be here," my brother whispered.

Tango chuckled. "Really? You're a tattoo artist slotted to have a booth here, and you didn't think they'd come try to harass you?" He shook his head back and forth. "Frankie, sometimes, I really think you did too many drugs in your early years or something."

"Hey!" I called out a little too loudly. "Don't talk about my idiot brother that way!"

"Gee, thanks, Liza." Frankie commented, sarcasm dripping from his words.

"Well, if you weren't an idiot, I wouldn't have to run away while you get to play house with the reason for this whole mess," I cracked out bitterly. Yeah, okay, so I didn't resent Michelle and the baby per se, but I did resent being sent away for their selfishness of wanting to be together without getting shit straightened out first. Michelle and my brother both made mistakes when they got together, the first of them being staying in Reno where the King's Demons ruled the city. My anger was warranted, since I was the only person who would suffer the consequences of their decisions.

Just as I was turning back to Tango, he reached out, grabbed my arm, and pulled me right up to his ridiculously large body. His hands tangled into my hair at the back of my head as he bent me backward and crashed his lips down on mine. I felt him kick his leg out a bit and heard my brother hiss out an "Ouch, motherfucker!"

"Okay, well, you're busy, so I'm gonna go hit my booth up for a while. Catch ya later about that technique you've been using," My brother called out while Tango's tongue found its way into my mouth when I gasped. Then he released my mouth only to dip his head into my side and nip my ear before whispering his message.

"Play nice, KDs are watching." That was all the permission I needed to let my hands do some exploring that my eyes had been able to do earlier. I took my time feeling all the dips and bumps of Tango's muscled body as our second kiss grew so heated, I was sure my panties would melt right off my body.

At twenty-four-years-old, I definitely wasn't a virgin. I'd had my fair share of kisses from men, but never in my life had one turned me so inside out and upside down. Dear, sweet, baby Jesus someone needed to save me, my panties, and my poor little starved-for-attention girl-parts. It was suddenly possible that I wouldn't survive running away with this man for protection, because holy hell, I had never felt such sizzling chemistry with another human being before.

7. LUCK BE A LADY
TANGO - 2 WEEKS, 6 DAYS AGO

I slowly peeled Frankie's sister from my body. There was no way I'd admit to myself that I did so reluctantly. The kiss was meant to be a distraction, but I couldn't stop reliving every possessive touch, the tingle when our tongues clashed, and the complete rush that flew through my body when our each of our mouths fought to conquer the other's. Never in my life had I felt that kind of instant, explosive chemistry.

I certainly hadn't felt it with Camilla, or else I might have fought harder – or at all – to preserve what we had before I deployed. It also didn't escape my notice that my feelings about the kiss might just be because I'd gone so long without that sort of touch in my life. It fucking sucked to admit that I was touch starved. That was a thing I'd heard one of the girls at the clubhouse talk about before. I shook the thought off and pulled my head out of my ass long enough to reassure the woman still tucked in my embrace.

"It's okay. They've moved on. When your brother left, they followed him." I felt her tense up immediately. "No need to worry. There are too many people around who know Frankie. They won't try anything more than delivering a verbal message while he's at the expo."

"That's good to know, but I wouldn't put anything past them. They snatched me up from campus when I was still in school." Now it was my turn to tense. Frankie hadn't told me details about what they'd done to her before, just that it hadn't been pretty.

"I really hope, for their sakes, that you meant a college campus. Not that snatching you, and doing whatever they did wasn't bad enough, but you weren't..."

"I was in college, not underage. Not that it would have stopped them. I honestly believe they didn't care how old I was at the time. I was nineteen, and I looked young for my age."

The gorgeous woman shrugged her shoulders as if it was no big deal. I knew that wasn't the case, but I didn't want to push anything here and have a potential outburst from her that could attract attention. I'd find out later, though. I'd also file that information away for future reference. We didn't run into too many King's Demons members in South Dakota, but there was always the chance with the Sturgis Bike Rally in August that brought bikers from all over the country, and even other parts of the world.

"We'll discuss all that later," I told her.

"Or we won't, because it's not necessary," she countered.

"It is necessary to know, so that my club understands how they operate and what to expect. We don't have dealings with King's Demons normally since they're over here in Nevada, Arizona, California, and New Mexico while our club runs up in the Dakotas and along the East Coast. We will have a conversation about what went down before, and I'll expect you to be completely transparent with us when we do."

She sighed and bit down hard on her plump lower lip while glancing up at me with those whiskey-colored eyes that had my attention the moment I first saw them. "Whatever you think will help," she finally conceded.

"I'm going to need you to help break everything here down for the night, and we're going to pack all the supplies to go for transport back to my shop, because I have a sneaking suspicion that I won't be able to finish out the weekend now that they've been spotted at the expo."

She sighed again, and the sound was pure defeat. "I'm so sorry you got dragged into my brother's mess, too."

I reached out and took hold of her chin, forcing her to look me in the eyes. "Don't worry about that shit. It's not on you."

"No, but my brother is affecting your business here, he's making me your burden, disrupting your life as well as mine. It's not fair."

"I could have said no, babe. I didn't. That makes all the rest of it on me. Now, help me pack up, and we'll go grab something to eat before we hit the hotel for the night."

"I didn't bring any of my things with me. Frankie said we were just doing introductions and that we wouldn't leave for a couple days."

"Don't worry about your stuff. I have a prospect with me that went to grab it."

"Won't they know I'm with your club if they see your

prospect going into my place? I'd bet money they have someone watching my place."

"Don't worry, he's a prospect so he's not allowed to have any club tats, and he won't be wearing his kutte either. He'll look like some asshole heading into your building and leaving with some luggage. He also hired a hooker to meet him there, so it'll look like he's leaving with his woman and not there for you." I winked at her when I let her in on that little secret.

She stared at me wide-eyed for a full minute before she started laughing. "You guys are too much! A hooker decoy? Oh my God!" Her laughter continued as she helped me pack up and I couldn't help the way that laugh of hers hit me right in the solar plexus and nearly stole my breath. I should have been worried because that was the type of feeling that couldn't be ignored.

8. DRIVING INTO THE FUTURE

TANGO - 2 WEEKS, 5 DAYS AGO

THE PROSPECT I BROUGHT WITH ME, ASHTON DAVIDSON, HOPPED A flight back to South Dakota, taking Liza's belongings with him as his baggage just in case he was tailed to the airport. He never made contact with the girl, so the King's Demons wouldn't have any reason to suspect she knew him or was headed his way. So far, it seemed to have worked out beautifully.

By the time I got the call from Frankie, letting me know that the KDs were back at the Expo and sniffing around the space I'd occupied the past two days, I knew we made the right decision. I also knew we had a good damn head start, since they assumed I'd show up again today. We left at five in the morning, and I was ever thankful the Prospect and I had driven the truck down, so I'd have a place for all the equipment that needed to be toted back. It would have been too damn cold for Liza on the bike, since I didn't think that she was used to riding. Sure, her brother had a motorcycle, and did his fair share of riding, but from what Liza had mentioned, she'd never ridden with him. I assumed it was because she didn't want to be near motorcycles or bikers in general thanks to her previous experience with the King's Demons MC.

"So, you never been on a bike?" I don't know why I felt the need to ask, but it was bothering me that she hated my world so much.

She smirked, and I only just caught it out of the side of my eye as we bumped down a road that hadn't been resurfaced in ages. Taking some back roads and deviating from the quicker route I'd normally take home, was done in an effort to keep the King's Demons from finding us too quickly. The first part of our plan was to lay low with the woman; the second part was to fight if necessary to protect her. Once Charlie overheard the guys talking about Liza's situation, it was all the woman could do to force Rage's hand to help Liza. It hadn't been too long ago that Charlie herself was on the run from her husband as well as his mistress. The bitch, who turned out to be Charlie's secret half-sister, had pulled the husband into a plot to murder his wife for the insurance money she would leave behind. He never even knew that it was also some sort of twisted revenge plot against Charlie, since she lucked out and was raised by her father while the sister had been raised by their crazy mom and a monster of a father.

Needless to say, a woman having to go in hiding was something of a trigger for Charlie, and now Liza had a champion on her side, even if she didn't know it yet.

"I never said I hadn't been on a bike before. I just said my brother never took me."

"When did you get to ride?"

Her smirk completely disappeared as a frown marred her otherwise beautiful face with a telling tightness that pulled Liza's lips in together and furrowed her brow.

"When I was nineteen," she explained. I remembered her saying that she'd been nineteen when the King's Demons got a hold of her once before.

"You don't have to tell that story yet," I reassured her. She was going to have to explain eventually, but I wanted her to feel comfortable with me before she did. I needed her to understand that I would only put her through retelling her horrible ordeal if it was absolutely necessary.

"I do, and we both know it. Might as well get it over with." She leaned back, getting comfortable on the beat-up leather seat of the old Chevy Blazer we occupied. "My brother has always had a stupid streak," she started her story, and I had to refrain from chuckling, having known her brother for quite a few years considering we ran in some of the same circles with the tattoo conventions. Plus, there was the fact that I was originally from Carson City. Moving in the same circles in the tattoo world while living that close was a given.

"He was into some even dumber shit back then. I'm pretty sure he had a coke habit he couldn't afford, but he also liked to gamble." She scoffed at the memory. "I think the gambling was originally just a means to an end. When it paid off, he could get more drugs. When it didn't, he was in need of way more money, and started playing for higher stakes. Unfortunately, he was playing for those higher stakes in one of the King's Demon's establishments. It was there that he lost really big for the first time. You know how these things go. He went somewhere else to try to win bigger in order to pay that debt off. Everything snowballed, and when those assholes came to collect, my brother was flat fucking broke and being evicted from his apartment."

Shit, now I understood how the sister had gotten involved in the first place. "He came to see you?" I asked the question, but I already knew the answer she was going to drop.

"He sure did. I was at the University of Nevada – Reno, living in the dorms when Frankie showed up. I don't know why he thought I'd have any money, but he asked anyway. Then he asked if he could crash for the night."

She sighed and glanced out the window for a long moment before she managed to continue. "The next day, I guess someone saw us leave the dorm together. I hugged him goodbye; he took off one way, I went the other, and never made it to class that day or for the rest of the week."

"So, someone threw you on the back of their bike and no one noticed you putting up a fight?"

"No, someone snatched me into a van that was waiting by the curb, and only after they bashed me over the head with something, a bottle I think. They knocked me out long enough to get me out of there without making much of a scene."

Liza nodded at the wide-eyed look I toss her way briefly as I continued to drive. Damn, but I wanted to pull over and wrap her in my fucking arms. I didn't understand why I felt that possessive need. It just felt right to comfort her while she told her story.

She moved her hand to just behind and above and her left ear, and shivered, as if a cool breeze just blew across her skin. The memory of her attack and imprisonment was clearly having an effect.

"Were you still in the van when you woke?"

I could tell from my peripheral vision that she shook her head. "I woke in a dingy room. The only furniture in the place was a nasty twin-sized mattress on the floor. You know the kind they put on kids' bunk beds?"

"Yeah, I know what you mean."

"Well, I was lying half on, half off one of those things in this room where the paint was peeling off the walls and there was enough dirt on the floor that I almost thought it was an actual dirt floor. I figured I was in an old root cellar or something. My head was a jumbled mess of pain and confusion, and I was so thirsty that my mouth was literally sticking together. I didn't remember being hit or stuffed into the van at first. I still don't remember being stuffed into the van, just that it was there.

"When the door opened, and more light poured in than what had been seeping through the crack under the door, my whole body locked up. Everything froze for a moment in a time before I took that next breath. Scuffed, dirty motorcycle boots came into view. The guy standing there moved forward a little then toed me in the ribs. I moved, inadvertently then, and his laugh skated across my skin like a thousand needles pricking me all at once. It was a thing that let me know I wouldn't be around much longer if I didn't play along and give into whatever it was he wanted from me."

"Was it Random?"

"No, it wasn't. It was his second in command, Vanquish, I think. I just know they mostly called him Van."

I nodded my head knowing exactly whom she was talking about, and dreading what was to come in her story, because a man like Van didn't leave young women untouched.

"Once he realized I was alive and awake, he reached down and grabbed me." Liza flinched with the memory and then curled in on herself. She wrapped her arms around her chest, as if to shield herself. It didn't take a genius to figure out the asshole must have grabbed her breast.

"When he realized I was still wearing a bra, he got angry, and started ripping at my shirt. He tore it off my body and then my bra was next. I started fighting back. I'd rather be dead, or at the very least passed out again, if I was going to have to go through what he was about to do to me."

She shook a little, making me wish I could stop her from having to relive whatever went down. The only thing that kept me from doing so was that I knew her brother had said she hadn't been raped. I wondered briefly if he'd just been given a watered-down version of events to spare him. Since Vanquish was in the picture, it was altogether possible.

"Since I was fighting back, he got rougher and slapped me as he kept trying to peel my bra from my body. He was laughing the entire time and telling me how he preferred when women put up a good fight for him. I punched him in the dick then, and he doubled over holding on to himself for a moment. I tried to get run past him to the door he'd come through, but before I could get too far, he reached out and grabbed my ankle. The dickwad yanked me back so hard that

I fell flat on my face and then he kicked me." Her whole body shook again with the memory. "I ended up with three broken ribs from those kicks. He had my pants down to mid-thigh before I finally found my voice, scratchy and dry as it was, I started screaming, and before he could get my pants down to my knees, another man came in and threw him off me.

"At first, I thought someone was there to save me. Then he started yelling at the Van guy and telling him they needed me to not look like I'd been through the ring just yet. I honestly thought they meant a boxing ring or something, but I found out later that wasn't the case."

"Sex slaves?" I asked, having heard the rumors of what those bastards were into. She nodded. "You meet some of them?"

She nodded again. "One." A far off look in Liza's eyes accompanied her single word. I let the rest of her story ride there with us for a few miles, unfinished.

"Was it Random?"

"Yeah, he was the one that came in and threw Van out. When he finally saw the damage that had already been done to me, he cussed, and basically threw a fit. Once he left the room, no one else came in for two days except this one slip of a girl who was barely wearing clothing, and what she wore was practically falling off of her body. There just wasn't enough meat on her bones to hold anything up. I felt so bad, until she told me they fed her just fine, she just refused to eat it, or when forced to do so, she would throw it all up immediately."

"What the hell?" I asked, not understanding why any woman would do that to herself.

"She was trying to look less attractive, so they'd let her go." Liza's soft voice spoke of a conversation she had with the woman that wasn't going to pass her lips again. I understood. Some things were best left locked away.

"You said that she was the only one allowed to come into the room where you were being kept for a while. Do you know how long you were there?"

"For the next two days, she was the only person I saw. I don't even know her name. She never would tell me. She told me that the girl with the name had died a long time ago, and she was just a body now. She nearly fainted in the room with me that second day, and after they took her out, I never saw her again. Then on the fourth day, Random came for me."

My whole body tightened at that statement. "Who took care of you after the girl left?"

"There wasn't anyone," she informed me.

"What about food, water?"

I noticed the slight movement, indicating she shrugged her shoulders. They'd left her alone in a room, with no food or water, for two days. My body began to vibrate with anger. "What happened when Random came to get you?"

She cleared her throat and then turned so that her body faced mine. "He took me to a room where a bunch of the guys were waiting. They were all in various stages of undress, and the fear of what was about to happen to me had me shaking inside and out. He took me to the center of the room, where they had this iron tool sitting on a table. They sat me in a chair, strapped my arms to the table, palms up, and then he used some kind of torch to heat up the end of the iron bar I'd seen. It was a brand." She rolled the sleeves of her hoody up and it was the first I'd seen the scars displayed there. One was placed right overtop of what must have once been a tattoo but was now a scar that stamped KDS into the once tender flesh of her forearm.

"It was just after they got through with the second one that Random got a call, and when he did, he looked angry, but conceded to whatever the caller wanted. Then, he scooped me up, held me in his arms all the way out of the warehouse we had been in, and he took me to his bike. He didn't say a word until he commanded me to get on. Then he told me, 'I'm taking you to your brother, so get the fuck on or go back in there and let my men enjoy what they're missing out on now.' He was referring to the club brothers of his that had been salivating over the pain those brands caused me."

"They branded you," I whispered while trying to contain my anger.

"They branded me as a slave of the King's Demons. That's what the KDS means. The girl who had been coming in to feed me, before she passed out, had them, too. I didn't realize that's what it was until after they branded me. If Random hadn't received that call, I don't know what would have happened to me. I think I'd resigned myself to going out just like the girl who had attempted to care for me, but I don't think I could have managed her slow demise. I'm sure I would have found a quicker way."

"He took you to your brother after that call? Did you ever find out from him what the call was about?"

She shook her head in the negative. "He told me he didn't know what I was talking about." I was about to ask another question, but Liza held up her hands to stop me. "He was lying. I know that much, but I could never get him to tell me what my brother promised them, or what strings he pulled to get me out of there. Random never said and neither did my brother."

"Looks like we need to have another chat with your brother."

"Good luck with that," Liza mumbled before she leaned her head back on the headrest and closed her eyes. It was obvious that reliving her ordeal at the hands of the King's Demons had left her needing a minute to get herself together. I could understand that, because if I were to see any of them riding near us after seeing what they'd done to her, I don't think I'd be trying to hide from them as originally planned. Instead, I'd be bowling for bikers with the truck until I took out enough of them to make me feel a little bit better about the situation.

Still, when we pulled over to gas up again, I took my phone out and filled Iceman in on what had gone down. He agreed with me that someone we trusted needed to go pick up Frank Rossi because he had information we were going to need. There weren't too many things that would make a club like King's Demons give up a branded woman. That was information we couldn't do without.

9. BUMPS IN THE ROAD
LIZA - 2 WEEKS, 2 DAYS AGO

HOME SWEET HOME WAS THE STUFF OF BIKER COMPOUND WET dreams apparently. When we rode into the parking area, after passing through a gate system, we were greeted by eight bikers, one woman, and more bikes than I could account for, if our welcome party were the only riders. That told me there were still a handful or two somewhere out of sight. Knowing there were more bikers hiding out somewhere made me nervous.

The minute Tango turned the truck off and stepped out, two of the bikers along with the woman who had bright red hair and a giant smile plastered to her face, damn near ran over to greet him. Hugs were banded about as if he'd gone off to war for months and just returned home. I was a bit confused by the dynamic, but assumed this was Whiskey and Fox, the best friends who Tango had served with. He told me about them on our three-day trip to South Dakota from Reno. I also assumed that the woman was the one the two guys apparently shared.

I still couldn't wrap my mind around that one, but to each their own. The woman, I think he'd said her name was Amy, stood up on tiptoes and attempted to plant a kiss on Tango's lips. He quickly dodged to the left, forcing her to land her thin lips on his cheek instead. I had to stifle a laugh, because he seemed annoyed by her attempted too-familiar kiss while she was put off by him not allowing it. The men he'd described as his best friends each gave the other a questioning glance as it happened to. I wondered if they were questioning her being so forward and familiar or his rebuff.

"Are you getting out of that truck any time today, lady?" One of the other bikers asked of me. He was older with paler skin than the men around him; short cropped blond hair, and alert, watchful blue eyes that were pinned on me. Glancing down, I noticed that his patch stated he was the President and that his road name was Iceman. I simply nodded to him, gathered the things I had in the front seat with me, and went to open my door. Tango beat me to it though, having made his way around to get the door and offer me a hand getting out. I took it, since the truck was on the high side. While I wasn't a tiny thing, I was still short enough that it was a task getting down when my hands were full of the shit that I'd just stupidly piled into them.

"Everybody, this is Liza Rossi, she's going to be staying with us a while until we figure out what to do about the situation with the King's Demons."

From what Tango had told me, he already informed his club about everything concerning my situation, including the details of my prior kidnapping by the KDMC. The redhead looked on questioningly as he spoke.

"If she's in trouble with another MC, why is she here?" The 'with you' seemed to be implied in the woman's question.

"That's club business," he damn near snapped at her. She stepped back, clearly affronted by how he spoke to her. Whiskey and Fox flanked her sides and scowled in Tango's general direction.

"It will remain club business only, for now, and until I say different," Iceman reiterated, as he too must have noticed the interactions concerning the other woman and her two men. The threesome continued to scowl as Tango tossed his arm around my shoulder and guided me to the front door of the building. Oddly enough, there were very few windows on the ground floor, which set my anxiety on edge.

"Come on, let's get you settled in with your things. Ashton brought your luggage already, so all your stuff is waiting on you." Tango explained as one of the other men stepped in front of us and did some bippity-boppity-boo shit to the panel on the door before it managed to open up. We all packed into a smallish room that barely contained all the large, hard-bodied bikers. Once again, another control panel was accessed before the next door was pushed open with a snick and hiss of air, leading into a huge, open floor room that looked like something you would find when walking into an old school honkytonk.

Wooden floors predominated the space. The far wall held a bar that ran damn near three quarters the length of the room. Beyond that, in a back corner, were several pool tables and other tabletop games. To my left, high-top tables surrounded a stage. There were a few couches and lounge chairs interspersed all willy-nilly, too. A set of stairs led up to a balcony that connected to what appeared to be a long hallway that seemed to match one right below it. The lower hallway was located between the stage and pool table areas, effectively splitting them into separate spaces within the large common area.

While I was surveying the space, it wasn't lost on me that there were bikers lounging about here and there. It seemed relatively laid back, but then again, it was only half passed two in the afternoon. According to Tango, things could get wild around the place, and they did have club whores that were generally known as sweetbutts. His club jokingly referred to them as BRATs. When I'd asked what BRATs meant, Tango had chuckled before informing that it meant 'Bitches Relinquishing Ass and Tits' or some such nonsense the oversexed idiots of his club had come up with.

All that really mattered was that each of the women who fell in that category were here willingly to service the members who chose to use them. Yes, I did throw up in my mouth a little when he described it. Mostly, because I remembered the girl with no name from when I had been taken by the King's Demons. She hadn't been willing to service anyone, and it made processing how a woman would consent to put herself in a similar situation very difficult to process. I couldn't wrap my head around the freedom aspect, after having my only interaction with that sort of situation coming from a dark and horrible place. None of the women I saw in the Aces High clubhouse, so far, appeared to be bothered by a single thing though.

The more worrisome thing was that I was receiving a few

appreciative looks from some of the men lounging about when Tango glared in the general direction of his President. "Did you send out the memo?"

"I did," he offered on a chuckle. "I told them hands off, that doesn't mean they can't appreciate the scenery, T." Tango grumbled something in response that I didn't quite catch, but it didn't matter, because he grabbed hold of my hand and pulled me to the right, and down one of two halls I hadn't even taken notice of yet. I'd been too busy orienting myself with the other half of the large space to realize there was so much more.

"Your room is down this hall for now, but I will be sure to get you moved over near mine as soon as possible."

"Why? What's wrong with this hall?"

"This is where the BRATs stay. We have some visiting members from another chapter in right now, so most of the rooms were taken up where the members and guests are usually placed since we haven't finished renovations downstairs yet."

"Will there be an issue with people trying to get into my room?" I asked the question quietly so as not to offend anyone, or give out ideas, but my words stopped Tango cold in his tracks.

"You know what? You're going to take my room for now. I can bunk with one of the guys or take this room down here for the time being, until the brothers from Cedar Falls head back home."

"I don't want to put you out," I argued. I had some money tucked aside. Maybe there was a hotel or something that I could get into.

"Fuck that! I'll never get any sleep if I'm worrying about some asshole trying to get in your room thinking you're another BRAT."

Just then the prospect I had seen briefly, and from a distance, in Reno strolled by. "Hey, Ashton, grab Liza's bags from the room you put them in, and bring them to mine."

Ashton's face grew a little pale as he glanced between Tango and me guiltily. Tango's back straightened and fists clenched, waiting for whatever the younger man had to say. It seemed neither of us were getting fuzzy, happy vibes from the prospect. Not that it had fuck-all to do with the man himself, but the impending bad news hung in the air like a stale fart, unwelcome and unrelenting.

"Well, I just came from there, and the thing is, I didn't have a key to the room when I went to put her stuff in there before." Oh damn, I already knew where this was going, and it made me sick to my damn stomach. Before he could say another word, one of their whores came out of a different room wearing my Vintage Rolling Stones t-shirt that my dad had given to me. It was an original t-shirt he had gotten for my mom many years ago, and she had never worn it, because it wasn't her thing.

"You thieving ass bitch, get my fucking shirt off your nasty ass body, right now!" I yelled, causing the entire room behind us to go dead silent. I did not give a single fuck though. That whore was wearing my shirt. It still had my mom's name on it, and was signed by Mick, himself.

"This isn't yours, you crazy cunt!" The woman screamed back at me.

"Turn around. I bet it says, 'To Katie, Love Mick" on the

back. "The Katie in question was my mom, since the shirt was signed for her specifically."

"Listen, you stupid whore, just because you don't know how to lock your shit up..." the girl started, but her eyes widened at something over my shoulder. I didn't bother to turn and look.

"What the fuck is going on here?" Iceman bellowed from somewhere behind me.

"I was just telling Tango that when I put Ms. Liza's things in the room meant for her, I didn't have a key, so I had to go find one."

"Why were you just now finding a key to the room today when you got back three days ago with her shit?" Iceman asked.

"Her things were in the brother's wing before, but when we got company, Rabbit told me to shift her room down here until they left," Ashton explained. "I brought her stuff down but didn't even think about the key situation until after I went to close the door and realized it's one of the two rooms down here with a key lock only."

That sent a chill straight through to my bones. It's a good thing Tango had already offered up his space, because I'd be damned if they put me in a room that could be locked from the outside with a key.

Iceman stepped in front of me, reached out, and turned the whore in front of us around so we could see the large, printed words on the t-shirt, just like I said there would be.

"Mother fucker!" he lamented, then snatched the shirt right off the bitch's body, leaving her naked from the waist up. He handed it over to me. "What the fuck else did you steal?"

The girl looked shell-shocked now with her big, fake tits on display. Though, she didn't seem to care about her semi-nudity. She was more concerned with Iceman's wrath. "I want every fucking bitch that works here out in this hallway. NOW! I don't give two fucks if you're in the middle of servicing a brother, get the fuck out here!"

"Oh shit," Ashton hissed under his breath. Doors opened and girls stepped out into the hall. Some were clothed, others weren't.

"Line up along the wall, now!" Iceman's command was heeded immediately. He stood opposite them along the other wall and eyed each of them momentarily before moving on. Then his gaze landed back on Tits Magee who had stolen my shirt.

"What else did you take? You've already stolen and attempted to lie to a brother and his guest. I'm warning you now, you do NOT want to add to your list of infractions."

"It's all sitting on my bed still, but honestly this was the only thing I took from that room. The rest was already out here in the hallway," she managed to get out on a whimper.

Iceman turned to me then. "Go with the prospect and check your things. Take note of anything you think may be missing, then come tell me." I did as he asked. When I came to the door of the room, it was obvious that I didn't have to go any further though. My bags were wide open, and there didn't appear to be anything left in them. The gasp that escaped me was answer enough.

"Those fucking cunts stole everything, down to my

underwear. Who the fuck steals another woman's panties?" I questioned, throwing accusing eyes their way. A couple of the women in the line flinched. Iceman took note and pulled them out.

"Get everything, and I do mean everything, you took from that room and bring it back in there now. Place what you took in a pile at your feet and wait there for me." Three girls, including the whore who had been wearing my shirt, scampered off to their respective rooms and began gathering things. Four more women stood there snickering.

One had the audacity to speak. "I told those skanks that shit wouldn't go over well. It would have been different if they each only took one thing, but greedy bitches get what's coming to them."

"And what the fuck did you take?" I scanned the woman, and noticed she was hiding her hands behind her back. I walked over and snatched at her arm to get her hand out from behind her body when the tink sound of a ring falling to the floor caught everyone's attention. I looked down to find my grandmother's ring. My father had hidden it in some luggage years ago, and there it was, rolling out to meet my feet in the hallway of the Aces High MC clubhouse.

I stooped to pick it up, and then stood and immediately slapped the whore who had the audacity to attempt to steal it. "This was sewn into a hidden compartment in my luggage by my late father. So, not only did you attempt to steal a family heirloom, you had to cut it out of my things."

The woman said nothing, just sneered at me as I stepped back. By now, the three women who had admitted to stealing things had already moved through the hallway, back to the room that was supposed to be mine, with arms full of my clothing and belongings. Another woman raised her hand. Iceman rolled his eyes at her gesture. "What Sheri-Baby?"

"Amber gave me some new shampoo and conditioner earlier, and some makeup that would match my complexion. I'm guess I now know where she got it, and why she was so willing to give it away." She glanced my way then. "I never used it, because I never trust a whore not to tamper with shit."

"I have the same rule. You can toss it all. I'll get new stuff," I told her. She nodded then offered me a small smile.

"I like that you weren't afraid to call all these cunts out for what they did." She turned back to Iceman then. "Amber was right. There were already things thrown out into the hallway when we came back in earlier. I ignored it, thinking someone was having trouble with their woman or a new girl was being hazed or something."

The blonde seemed like a sweet girl. She definitely wasn't shy, but she had a somewhat soft-spoken demeanor that made me wonder why she was here. I guess I had pictured the club women to be more like the ones who had stolen my things, like the hardened biker bitch, Amber, and there was no room for any exceptions.

"Let's go see if that's everything returned," Iceman said as he indicated for me to move into the room. He turned to the prospect before following behind me. "Make sure no one out here moves until we're done."

"Sure thing, Iceman."

It took more than fifteen minutes to go through everything while trying to remember what exactly I had packed to bring with me and what I didn't. I knew all the important things, and they were all accounted for again. Despite being happy to have everything back, I separated all the underwear from the pile of my belongings. No fucking way in hell would those things touch my body again, even after washing. Nope. Nope. Nope. I pointed to the pile.

"You can burn the underwear, because the fuck if I'm putting them back on my body. There's not enough bleach in the world."

"You little..." one of the whores seethed. I couldn't see which one, but it didn't matter, because Iceman shut her down, and let me know exactly who had spoken.

"Shut it, Amber!"

"It looks like all my important things are back. I can't honestly remember what I packed and what I didn't when it comes to the more generic stuff, so the best I can tell you is this looks about right." I shrugged as I scrunched my nose in distaste over the fact that some nasty bitches had their grubby little paws all over my stuff. It was just one more fucking problem my brother caused.

"Okay then," Iceman leaned out into the hallway. "Cass, get in here," he called. The other three women who had brought my stuff back willingly when asked were already standing near the door, so Iceman crooked his finger at them to come inside. When the final woman showed up, I realized she was the one who had taken my ring. Once she was in the room with the other three, Iceman started talking.

"You four have fifteen minutes to pack your shit and get the fuck off club property. Honor and loyalty are a hallmark here. If we can't trust you, you don't stay. You were all warned when given a room here. It was explained to you that you would treat our guests as you would our brothers. You stole from our guest, so that means you would steal from a brother."

"We thought she was another sweet butt," Cass snipped back sassily.

"Sweet butts are our guests, too. Just because you're paid to be here doesn't make you any less of a guest. You steal from anyone while living under my roof and you'll find that you need to get the fuck out. Be glad I'm giving you a minute to pack, because now I have to wonder what else you have in your rooms that you took without permission."

He turned to another brother then who had come in on the tail end of what was going on. "I want a brother or prospect on each of the four of them until they are off the property. Get Mech to remove them from the system too."

"Sure thing, Ice," the gorgeous blond man said before turning to me with a smirk. "Should be interesting having you around. Rage's woman got rid of two BRATs when she first showed up. You just tore down her record with 4 gone in under an hour." He slapped his hands together and rubbed them while laughing. "Ah, the entertainment."

"Go fuck off, Rabbit!" Tango told the man with a chuckle. "Don't listen to him. You didn't make any of this happen. They did this to themselves. That's not on you, babe." I nodded and started scooping my things back into the suit-cases. I sure as fuck was not going to feel guilty that some thieving ass whores were getting the boot from the club.

"We're gonna need to put a call out for more girls real

soon," Iceman told Rabbit as they both left the room. "The guys are going to get restless. Call Spinner and see if any of Rosy's girls want to come over. I know a few of them were chomping at the bit to switch things up a while back." I didn't hear the rest of their conversation as they walked out of range.

Once I had all my stuff zipped up in my luggage, I turned to see Tango watching me. "That everything, babe?"

"Yeah, I'm going to need new toiletries. Like Sherry-Baby said out there, I don't trust a whore with shit. No way in hell am I using shampoo they might have dumped hair remover in." He laughed and nodded in understanding.

"We'll take a ride out to town and hit up a store for you once we get this stuff moved. I'm fucking sorry you had to put up with this shit first thing. You're supposed to be here for protection and this shit makes it look like we can't do our fucking jobs on that count."

"It's okay. Obviously, you had a bit of problem with sticky-fingered skanks here. Glad I could help weed them out for you. I feel like you guys got a little repayment for taking on my brother's problems now."

Tango smirked and grabbed both of my suitcases. I followed along behind him and kept my eyes glued to his muscular back and shoulders the whole way. It didn't stop me from noticing the Amy woman glaring at me as we passed by her. She was literally sitting on two men's laps as we moved beyond them, and yet she was giving me the stink-eye over Tango leading me around the clubhouse. That was just strange. At least, I thought it was, until I saw her back. She had a kutte on like many of the men, only hers had a banner thing across the top that said "Property of WTF" and one across the bottom that said Aces High – Dakotas Chapter.

What the fuck, indeed, because it didn't take a rocket scientist to put together the three best friends, Whiskey, Tango, and Fox equaled WTF. I waited until we got to Tango's room to ask him personally.

"Is that Amy woman your old lady too?" The weird, quizzical look on Tango's face made me think my question was silly for a moment. That moment didn't last long, though.

"No, why would you ask that?"

"Her Kutte had 'Property of WTF' written on it. I thought that stood for you and your two buddies that you told me about."

"No, her property patch says W plus F." He said it so nonchalantly that I didn't think to question it anymore.

"Looks like WTF. They might want to get that fixed so there's no confusion, considering you told me everyone calls you three WTF collectively."

"Yeah, I guess so," he offered.

"Do you have an old lady? Is someone going to come to your room looking for you later, and want to kick my ass for being here?"

Tango laughed. "Nope. I haven't been with a woman in almost two years. Nearly made the mistake of asking a cheating girlfriend to marry me. Thankfully, she let me know what she was about before I pulled the ring out."

"Shit, that's rough! I guess I can understand the hiatus then."

"What about you? Are there any boyfriends, fiancés, or a husband being left in the dust after your brother screwed you over?" It was my turn to laugh.

"Definitely not," I muttered.

"Why *definitely* not?"

"I've dated here and there over the years, so don't get me wrong when I say this, but the shit I went through when I was nineteen left me undatable for the most part."

"What do you mean? Were you too traumatized?" His voice was full of concern as he asked.

"No, nothing like that. It's just that locals in Reno wouldn't go near me because I'd been marked by those assholes as their property. The few men from out of town who would date me weren't there long enough to make a go of anything. Those who decided to stick around, and there were only two over the years, were quickly run out of town once they found out what the marks on my arms meant. I tried to live a normal life in spite of what happened to me, but someone in that fucked up MC didn't want me to have an ounce of happiness." I sighed.

"So, the punishment you got for your brother's bullshit years ago never really ended?"

"No, I guess in a way, it didn't." We managed to make it all the way up the stairs, down the hall, and to the third door on the right from the balcony area overlooking the goings-on down in what I'd heard referred to as 'the commons' by the time our conversation drifted to a close.

"This is my room," Tango explained as he unlocked the door. "Well, it'll be yours until the other guys leave and we can get you one on this same hall."

94

"Thank you." I hoped he understood just how genuine that sentiment was, because I truly meant it. He didn't have to get involved, or get his club involved with rescuing me from my brother's bullshit. He left a tattoo convention early to get me out of town faster, and then the man had to give up his personal space for me.

"Can I ask you something, and you not think I'm a total nutcase?"

He chuckled. "I guess that depends on what you're asking."

"You know my history. Do you think...?? I glanced around noting the bed was a King size and there was a small loveseat tucked up under the windowsill. Perfect. "Do you think you could stay in this room with me until mine is ready. I just..." I stopped short trying to form my thoughts into words. "Logically, I know you're trying to help me, and that you guys aren't like King's Demons. Hell, what your president just did with the women who stole my things proved that. I still, um... it's just that all the bikers... it makes me nervous being here." Okay, so that wasn't the most eloquent way to basically say I'm quaking in my boots, but it apparently got the job done.

"You don't need to explain anything. I'll hit up the couch," he nodded to the loveseat.

"Um, no. I'm five feet, five inches. I think I can fit on that just fine. Whereas you're what? I'm guessing six-three or more?"

"I'm six-four, and it wouldn't be the first time I passed out there, so it's no big deal, really."

"Whatever. Please, don't argue. I'll feel better this way.

Besides, I'm liable to have some nightmares considering all the triggers in my life at the moment, so you better get all the good sleep you can right now."

The rest of the night, and the next day, proved much less stressful as Tango took me shopping for the things I needed to replace, and we settled into a quiet little routine of splitting bathroom time and dancing around one another like we'd been in each other's lives for years instead of only five days. We had already been sharing a hotel room for three nights, so that was probably why it seemed so familiar sharing a room with him in the compound, too. If I was being honest with myself, I wasn't sure how I was going to cope when I was able to get a room all to myself. Worse, I didn't think I wanted to be without Tango. I may have only known him for less than a week, but the connection I felt with him was undeniable.

10. STAKING A CLAIM
LIZA - 2 WEEKS AGO

A KNOCK ON THE DOOR TO THE ROOM I SHARED WITH TANGO startled me. I hadn't expected anyone to check up on me after he'd gone to his tattoo shop, Liquid Lines, earlier in the day. He had some appointments set that he couldn't reschedule, and while I offered to go, he refused. Apparently, it was a security issue to have me outside the compound too much. Then there was the tattoo shop connection, considering he'd had a booth at the convention in Reno.

I understood, even If I didn't like it very much. I flipped a robe over my pajamas that consisted of boxer shorts and a tank top, since I hadn't yet replaced everything that I refused to wear after the whores had stolen my things. The boxers had been courtesy of Tango's dresser drawer, where I pilfered the pair with permission.

"Who is it?" I asked as I moved closer to the door.

"It's me, Amy." I recognized her voice immediately and cringed as I moved closer to the door. I honestly didn't want to be in a room alone with the woman. I still hadn't figured out the dynamics between her, Whiskey, Tango, and Fox. It seemed like Tango thought one thing was going on while the other three were under the impression that he was part of her all-male harem somehow. It did not leave me with an easy-breezy feeling, nor did the looks I caught her throwing my way whenever I was in the common area with Tango.

I slipped the door open a crack and plastered a polite smile on my face. "Tango isn't here right now. He went to the shop."

"I know," was all she said as she stared me down, waiting for something. I stood there watching her, watching me. "Are you going to let me in?" she finally snapped the question at me after our minutes-long stare down.

"Um, no," I stated plainly. Her jaw dropped in surprise, and I giggled on the inside at the reaction. She really thought I'd just welcome her into a room that technically wasn't even mine. No way.

"May I ask why not?" she finally managed to sputter a bit indignantly.

"Tango isn't here. This is *his* space. I wouldn't feel right inviting you, or anyone else, in when I'm not certain how he would feel about you being in his private space."

"You are in his private space!" she huffed at me, as if that meant something.

"He invited me into his room. He's not here to invite you," I explained slowly. Not that I should have to, as that seemed like common sense to me.

She was getting frustrated, as evidenced by the uptick in her respiration, and the slight pink tinge to her cheeks and neck. "I don't understand why you're being difficult. Tango and I have an intimate relationship, of course I'm always invited into his room."

Her use of the words 'intimate relationship' was purposely said as a way to inform me that they had sex. I thought back to him saying he hadn't had a woman in more than two years, and I wondered now if he meant sexually, or just a relationship. It didn't matter either way, as it as none of my business, no matter how much I wished that were different. Amy, however, seemed to want me to think she had something more than just sex going on with Tango. Weird that he hadn't been around her much, outside of being in the common room at the same time, since we got back from Reno. I would expect a man who had been away for a few days to be raring to go with a woman, if they were in a relationship and he'd been gone for any length of time.

"Look, Amy, I don't know you. I don't know your history. I only know what Tango has confided in me, and that hasn't been much where you're concerned. He said the four of you – along with Whiskey and Fox – were friends, and that's fine. When he's here, you're more than welcome to come see him in his room. But when he's not, you need to wait for him to get back.

"I came to speak to you," she hissed between tightly gritted teeth. Yep, clearly frustrated with me.

"You are speaking to me," I informed her.

She looked over her shoulder and down both lengths of the hall. I did as well, and there was only one person there who was doing a horrible job of pretending not to eavesdrop. The sexy blond guy they called Rabbit was watching us curiously with a grin on his face.

"I meant in private," she informed me rather snarkily.

"Well, give me a moment to get dressed and I can come to your room then. Which room is it?" I asked her as she lost her absolute shit.

"Are you retarded or are you trying to piss me off?" Rabbit looked like he was about to jump in and save me. I shook my head slightly and he settled on simply glaring at the woman as he blatantly watched the show she was putting on.

"Well, sweetheart, that is so not the fucking way to get me to have a damn conversation with you. I'm sorry you're not getting into Tango's room like you wanted, but again, that's for him to decide. If respecting someone's property makes me retarded, then I guess I am. If you truly wanted to speak with me in private, I'm sure there are plenty of other places that conversation can happen, but it will not be in *this* room." I stood my ground, and she was boiling over with red-faced rage, and not at all happy that I was maintaining my cool under pressure.

"Tango and I are together," she stated.

"Does he know that? I thought you were with the other two guys?" I questioned, making her steam a little more with each word I muttered.

"We are all together!" she damn near yelled through still gritted teeth. I honestly felt like she might crack a molar if she kept it up. Also of note, I was beginning to think there was something to that whole red hair and fiery temper stereotype. I noticed that Rabbit was on his phone at that point while continuing to keep watch on what was going on with us in the hallway.

"He already told me that you're all friends, but honey, honestly, I wouldn't let any of the other guys in here either without his permission. It's Tango's room. If he wants guests, he can decide when and who gets in when he's around to approve it. If what you really want is a conversation with me, then you can be polite and invite me to have a conversation with you. What I do not have to do is indulge you when you're being a complete twat and losing your temper with me for no good reason."

"What's going on here?" The man, who I learned was Whiskey, asked as he walked up with Fox quickly following behind him. I didn't get a chance to speak, because that was when Rabbit stepped in and hushed Amy as she attempted to shout her side of things at them.

"I'm not sure what your girl is doing here," Rabbit started to say.

"It's Tango's room. She's allowed to be here if she wants to be," Whiskey announced.

"No, she's not. He has a guest staying with him, and when he's not here to okay it, she shouldn't be coming around demanding entrance." Both Whiskey and Fox bounced their visual fields between Rabbit, me, and a still enraged Amy.

"What has you so upset, Ames?" Whiskey asked while Fox kept his eyes glued on me, suspicion filling them to the brim.

"I tried to come have a chat with this woman, but she's being so difficult. She refused to let me into T's room. She refused to speak to me privately, and she's been a horrible, condescending bitch the entire time." Amy whined to the men in her life as if I had poked holes in her very delicate feelings. Both Whiskey and Fox snapped their attention back to me then, glaring all the while. I simply stood there and rolled my eyes at her dramatics.

"No, that is not how shit just went down, and I would know because I've been standing in the hall watching since this one," he pointed at Amy, "knocked on that door." He then went on to explain exactly what had taken place, and both men suddenly dropped their gazes to the woman who had them wrapped around her manipulative little fingers.

"Why does it matter so much that you talk to Liza in Tango's room? Why not somewhere else, since she offered to do that?"

"Because it does!" She stomped her foot. Legitimately stomped it like a toddler while her arms were crossed over her chest in a defensive gesture.

"Why Ames?"

"Because I need to see what's going on in there. He's been so distant since he came back, and now she's sleeping in his room with him. Is he being unfaithful to us?"

I couldn't help it when I started to laugh. All of them turned to look at me then. Rabbit was the only one who attempted to contain his own humor at the situation. The other two men looked as aggrieved as Amy at her suggestion.

"Seriously? Is he cheating? You have two men standing right there who have claimed you as their own, and you want to know if a third man is cheating? That's rich!" I continued laughing, and they all went back to ignoring me while the two men focused their energy back on Amy.

"Amy, he wasn't all here before he left for the expo, you

know that. I'm not sure what's going on with T right now, but I don't think he was on the same page as the rest of us, sweetheart." Fox explained to her, trying to be kind about it.

"He was, I know he was. We talked all the time." She had serious crocodile tears welling up in her eyes. Fox moved forward and tucked her into his chest. I rolled my eyes at the move. If he wanted to be a sucker for a woman who was pining away for a different guy, then that was on him.

"Come on, Amy, Liza isn't the person you need to have that conversation with. We need to all sit T down and get answers straight from the source."

"Why is she here?" I heard her ask as they moved the woman away from the door, and further down the hall.

"That's club business," Whiskey told her.

"Bullshit. If it were just club business she wouldn't be sleeping in his room. Tell me the truth. Did he go find a woman to bring back? What did I do to make him so angry?"

"Amy..." One of them sighed her name in clear exasperation. "Let's talk about this at home, sweetheart."

"Why isn't he staying there with us? You guys never told me before..." Her whining was getting on my last nerve, and I was glad when they got her inside a room toward the other end of the hall before shutting the door so I could no longer hear her whining.

I rolled my eyes once more and glanced at Rabbit who was staring at me with something akin to awe in his eyes. "I just want you to know that the kind of loyalty you just showed for Tango, by not letting anyone in his space when he wasn't around, won't go unnoticed around here. If anyone, including any of those three, bother you again and

Tango isn't around, I want you to call or text me right away, okay?"

"Sure," I told him as I pulled my phone out and we exchange numbers. "Thanks for having my back with the truth. I have a feeling I would have been facing a lynch mob if you hadn't been here."

"No need for thanks, but I do believe you're right. I'm going over to Rosy's but I'll stop in at Liquid Lines and let Tango know what went down today. That way he'll hear it from an impartial third party."

"Thanks, again," I told Rabbit and then watched as he walked away and took the steps down to the first floor. I turned and marched my butt right back in the room I had been protecting like a fierce momma bear hiding her cub from danger. I have no clue why that woman wanted in Tango's room so badly. I'm guessing it had to do with being nosey since I was in the room, but I hated assuming things so I would wait and talk it over with Tango when he got in.

11. THE TRUTH
TANGO - 2 WEEKS AGO

ONCE RABBIT TOLD ME WHAT HAPPENED WITH LIZA AND AMY AT the clubhouse, I figured I better make it a short day. I finished up my last appointment at two o'clock and headed back to the clubhouse. Technically, I should have stayed open for walk-ins, but it was my business. I could run it the way I saw fit. When I got back to the clubhouse, the commons was already filling with people thanks to the fact that we had visitors from the Cedar Falls Chapter of the MC.

I knew they'd be visiting for a few days, because some of the older members came to meet, or get to know Charlie all over again. Her dad had been a member named Brazen, but he took her away from the club at her dying mother's behest when she was young. She found her way back to the club recently looking for a job and protection when her husband tried to have her killed.

Charlie ended up falling for our Vice President, Rage, and she stuck around long enough to become his Old Lady. She was a sweet woman who didn't take shit form anyone, kind of like someone else who recently fell into our lives. I bet that Charlie and Liza would get along really well and hoped to introduce them once the novelty with the Cedar Falls guys wore off.

In the meantime, I had a woman to go find, since Amy gave me no choice but to explain the situation and my past with Whiskey, Fox, and their Old Lady. It didn't take long to find her. She was in our room, working on something in Photoshop on her laptop. She didn't have internet access here, because of our security setup, and her not being granted access yet, but I had explained to her that if she gave me instructions, I could transfer the images from a USB drive to e-mail for her clients from a secure space off site.

"Hey, Liza," I called out to her. She smiled up at me beautifully.

"Hey yourself. I'm almost done with this set of images. I'm going to add them to the USB drive along with instructions on where to send them and with what message. I really appreciate you working with me to make sure my work doesn't suffer for having to be in hiding. Some of it I can put off, but I had a few deadlines that can't be missed because people are counting on me."

"I understand that babe. It's no problem." I set my messenger bag down on the chair in the corner and then glanced back over at her again. "Can you pause for a few minutes, so we can talk about what happened today?"

"Sure. Give me just a second to save everything as is, and..." her tongue poked out at the corner of her mouth where it was held in place by teeth that bit gently down on it.

I couldn't help smiling at the picture she made when she was 'focused' on something.

"Okay... And... Done." She closed her laptop, set it aside, and then gave me her undivided attention. I moved to sit beside her on the bed where she'd been working.

"So, Rabbit came by and told me what happened. I wanted you to know that he didn't hold anything back, including the part where she tried to be dramatic and pretend more was going on from your side than there was." He shook his head. "Honestly, that's not like her at all, so I'm not really sure where that was coming from."

"It was coming from jealousy and nosiness," Liza stated with a shrug.

"What?" I questioned.

"She made certain to tell me that the two of you were in an intimate relationship, and that she could come into your room whenever she wanted, but the emphasis was on your intimate relationship."

I don't know why it bothered me so much that Amy told Liza that. Mostly, because I didn't see myself as being in any relationship with Amy beyond friendship, and now I was going to have to explain the intricacies of what had gone down between us to Liza. Again, I don't know why. I just felt compelled to set her straight, so she didn't think I was taken.

I took in a deep breath and let it out before I started. "Amy and I have never been anything more than friends. I've wondered, based on things she's done and said a few times recently, if she thought there was more, but I swear to you, I thought I set her straight."

"You have clearly been had a sexual relationship of some

sort with her," Liza stated instead of phrasing it as a question.

There was no holding back as I launched into my history from the beginning. Liza only interrupting at the end. "So, let me get this straight, you have only ever received a few blow jobs from Amy during group activities with the other two guys, and somehow that translated into an intimate relationship for her?"

"Maybe, she factored in how close I was with Whiskey and Fox before we met her, and she assumed our closeness would instantly transfer to her, too. Truthfully, they all assumed I wanted a bigger role than they were casting me in with their sexcapades. That's a guess on my part because it isn't something any of us have sat down and talked about. I suppose that's something I am going to have to address with them, because what happened today won't be happening again."

I sighed and leaned forward with my elbows on my knees and my head sunk deep into my hands. "What Amy did today was out of line, uncalled for, and I am definitely not comfortable with her just coming into my room whenever she pleases. That's the whole point in putting a lock on the door. Amy coming to you about my private life, when she should have come to me, is my number one concern right now. Then there's the demand to get in my room. Amy has never been invited into my room before. Ever. The guys have brought her in here a few times without my permission. They just assumed it would be okay. To be honest, on the few occasions that happened, I usually left and went to stay in my office at work. Since Amy moved to Spearfish, they rented a little cabin near town that they all stay in together unless there's a need for them to be close to the clubhouse. I didn't think the surprise visits to my room would still be an issue, especially with you here."

"Well, I feel much better about not letting her, or anyone else, into your room then. I was a little worried that you might be mad at me for denying her, but honestly, I had no way of finding out since we haven't exchanged numbers."

"I can't believe I haven't done that with you yet," he groaned, as if to chastise himself for the slip. "I was the one who got you the burner phone to use." He shook his head. "I blame exhaustion after our trip. I'm usually more on my game."

"Oh, so normally, you don't forget to get the chick's digits that you spend a few days in hotel rooms with?" I joked.

"Well, when I don't think she'll be far from my side, it seems unnecessary." He winked. "I guess, today proved me wrong though."

"Yeah, but Amy has your number, right?"

"She does," he admitted.

"Then she could have called to verify if she belonged there, but she didn't because she knew she had never been allowed in your room like that on her own before."

"I suppose that was part of what was bothering her when she found out you were staying here, considering she'd never been allowed inside without Whiskey and Fox escorting her. Not that I ever specifically had to turn her away from my room. It never came up before, and honestly, I couldn't think of a reason she'd need to be here other than to talk. We can do that anywhere. It doesn't have to be in my personal space."

"I completely understand that. I offered to go somewhere else to talk to her, but she just got angry with me and thought I was being an asshole about things. I was taken by the King's Demons because someone was watching me, and the place where I lived. Also, there was a girl in the dorms who had run her mouth about me when the KDs started asking around after they saw my brother go into the dorm to look for me. If she hadn't given away personal information about me, maybe they would have just thought I was some random stranger he was talking to, and wouldn't have snatched me up that day? I might have noticed that I was being followed instead of walking into an ambush. So, privacy, and not giving information away to people, is a really big deal to me."

I moved closer and wrapped my arm around her shoulder, pulling her into my side.

"I promise, that will not happen this time."

"I trust you," she whispered and her warm breath teased at the side of my neck. "I don't know why, but I do." I kissed the top of her head then. It was the same gesture I'd made with Amy numerous times over the past eight or nine months since she'd been involved with Whiskey and Fox, but for some reason, it felt different as I pulled Liza in closer to me and hugged her. She felt right being there in my arms, like a part of myself that I'd been waiting to be reunited with. Christ, I sounded like a complete idiot inside my own head.

"It feels good to have told you the whole story about

what's been going on with my boys and Amy. It's been weird for me, because the guys I would usually talk to about this kind of shit are the same ones I don't feel like I can talk to anymore since they met Amy. They keep pushing for me to be a part of whatever it is they have going on. I know they think it will fix a broken part of me, but I never saw myself as broken. I just didn't have the urge to go find someone to replace Camilla right away."

"What happened with Camilla?" she asked. There was no expectation in her voice, though. She would be okay if I told her that I didn't want to talk about it, just as she would with listening to yet another of my stories. "I know you said you were going to ask her to marry you before you found out she was cheating, but how did that all come about?"

"Sorry, you're so easy to talk to that I forgot I hadn't really explained the whole scenario." So, I told her the story, and she sat and listened with her head on my shoulder and my arm wrapped around her, our sides touching completely from tip to toe. It was the first time I'd talked about my past without feeling it rip through me. It wasn't the loss of Camilla that had killed my spirit so much as coming home from being shot at only to have the woman I thought I loved betray me in the worst way.

"So, the funny part is, after it was all said and done, Camilla found out that this Pablo guy had two other fiancés in the area, too. Her sisters called me and texted relentlessly. They begged me to forgive her and take her back. She did, too. I ignored all of it."

"Whoa! So, she cheated on you, and at your welcome

home get together, after you had sex, she told you that she got engaged to another man, and then she thought you'd take her back after all that? That was ballsy!"

I chuckled. "Yeah, it was. Didn't work out for her either way, but I consider it karma for the way she treated our relationship. I'll never understand why people cheat. If your relationship isn't working, you either work to fix it, or you get out of it before you betray someone's trust. You owe it to each other to make sure you do one, the other, or both before you fucking move on to someone else, though. It's a matter of respect for everyone involved, including you. And if the other person isn't demanding that respect from you, chances are they aren't as into the situation as you think they are. Nobody wants to seriously take on a person who still has their baggage unpacked on another person's floor.

She tipped her head up and smiled so perfectly at me that my fucking heart skipped a goddamned beat in my chest.

"I couldn't have said it better myself." She sighed. "I guess your friends are playing a different game altogether though. I can't wrap my head around sharing a person the way they do." She shook her head into my shoulder.

"I think their dynamic is a bit more than just two guys sharing one girl. They won't admit it outright, but there's more to the triangle than just that."

"You think the guys have their own thing, too?" she asked.

"I think Amy acts as a buffer that lets what they feel for each other be okay."

"Do you think they're using her as a beard?" she asked, but before I could answer, she shook her head and disregarded her own comment. "No, that's not right. I saw how protective and defensive of her they both were. I think she's more the catalyst that ramps up the fire they have for one another. She adds the spark that ignites them." Liza nodded her head, as if affirming her own words were correct.

"I think that's exactly right," I agreed.

"I wonder why she's so hung up on needing you in the mix, too? I mean, aren't two guys enough? I can't imagine having two hot and horny dudes after my ass all the time, and then still demanding a third to hop into the mix. Her va-jay-jay must get tired at some point." I laughed along with her as she mentioned the last bit.

"I wouldn't know, since I never had actual intercourse with her."

"Maybe that's why she's so hung up on you, because she hasn't had a taste." Liza giggled then, and it was the best sound I'd heard in a while. "Wait, that's the wrong thing to say. She has had a taste; she just hasn't had you stick it to her in other ways yet. Maybe she feels shortchanged since you were always receiving and never giving?"

"I don't know. It feels good to have someone I can talk to about the whole mess without feeling pressured to join in with them, or feeling judged by others for what I have or haven't done."

"You think the other guys judge you?"

"It's human nature to judge, but not in the way you mean. I think they just wouldn't understand, because they assumed we were all one unit, and every time I've tried to talk to them about me not being a part of that, aside from an occasional romp, they all just give me that, 'sure pal,' look that I hate. So, I stopped trying."

"And that meant that you had no outlet for your frustrations."

"Yeah. My outlet became getting away from here as much as possible. If I wasn't working to set up Liquid Lines, I was out on runs for the club."

"I know club business is what it is, but could you tell me about what going on runs means, generically speaking? You guys aren't running people, drugs, or other illegal shit, are you?"

I smiled down at the concerned look in her eyes. "Not in the way you're suggesting. We do a lot of private security work. If a shipment moving via truck is carrying items that may be a high target item, we move with it as added security. Sometimes we're hired out as bodyguards, other times it may be to guard a warehouse between shipments."

"Ah, I get it. Muscle for hire, and the patches are an intimidation factor."

"Yeah, but we run other legitimate businesses here, too. We have the strip joint in town, Renegade Rosy's. Then there's my tattoo shop, Liquid Lines. There's an auto body shop in town that's owned and serviced by the club, too. Each member who owns those businesses takes the lions share, but they also employ other club members, and a portion of profits go back into the club to help another brother establish their own business. We all take turns doing our part on the security end of things as well, so no one gets burned out or too overtaxed to do their own jobs."

"That sounds like the best system ever. The fact that you help support the next endeavor, and they in turn help support the next. That's awesome."

"That's a true brotherhood."

"You guys are changing my minds about motorcycle clubs. I didn't think I'd ever look at someone wearing a kutte as a good person."

"The true assholes, that would hurt women, are the minority, Liza. I promise you that." She nodded, and while I'm sure she was still uncertain of the validity of that statement, at least her opinions about my guys were starting to turn around more and more. Though, I was sure the little incident with Amy wasn't helpful in that regard. I would be addressing that with my friends later.

Just as I was thinking that, my phone pinged. I moved away from Liza in order to grab it from the nightstand, where I'd tossed it earlier. A couple texts had come through while we were talking, but I'd been so lost in my conversation with Liza that I hadn't heard any until the last.

A group chat with Whiskey, Fox, Amy, and myself had popped up.

> Amy: I just want to say that I'm sorry for the scene today. I really only wanted to talk to her.

> Whiskey: You don't need to apologize.

> Fox: It's ok darlin'. You're all good.

Ten minutes had apparently gone by since the initial text.

Amy: Are you seriously not going to say
anything, T?

Well, shit, she was going to force some ugliness out of
me. I must have sighed out my frustration or grunted or
whatever, because Liza sat up straighter. "Is everything
okay?" she asked cautiously.

"Yeah," I told her as I angled the phone so she could see
the conversation. She rolled her eyes in response, but kept
her mouth shut. I had to admire that, because if I were in her
shoes, I'd probably have a whole lot to say considering she
was most definitely owed an apology. I smiled at her reassuringly.

Tango: I've been busy trying to explain your unusual reactions to Liza. She's going through some serious shit and didn't need you coming at her like you did today. It's not your business what her deal is here, but it is my business to tell you to keep your distance until you can apologize for your behavior and act like she's someone your friend gives a shit about. She's not some club whore to be treated like ass by you, or anyone else. And I don't give a fuck what Whiskey or Fox just placated you with, you damn sure do owe her an apology for being a jerk while she was being considerate as hell and loyal to me. She didn't know you. She didn't know if you were allowed in my space. Hell, I've never once – since I've known you – invited you into my space, so I don't know why you would think it was okay to go there without Whiskey and Fox being the ones to bring you. Especially since I wasn't even around. And they shouldn't be bringing you to my room without permission either. That's something I've been meaning to address with all of you since before Liza got here. We'll talk about this later, in person, and not through text.

I had angled the cell so that Liza could read over my shoulder as I typed, but she hadn't invaded my privacy to do so. That spoke volumes of her character.

"You can read my response, babe. You need to know that I have your back just as much as you had mine covered today." I handed her the phone and as she read it, I could have sworn I saw a sheen of tears in her eyes. She handed the phone back with a small smile and hopped off the bed.

"Thank you for that, but I'm still sorry to be mixed up in the middle of drama with your very best friends."

"None of that was your fault, so don't take that burden on those beautiful shoulders of yours. They're heavy enough with the rest of your worries."

"I'm going to shower and then go try to find something to eat. I haven't been out of this room since last night." That was a little alarming, since I didn't even get back until mid-afternoon.

"Babe, you don't have to be afraid to leave the room when I'm not here. I promise, no one here will harm you." Although, after being ripped into by someone who was supposedly my friend, in the doorway of our room, I could understand her reluctance. Fuck!

Another ping indicating another text came through.

Whiskey: Good job asshole, she's crying again.

Fox: That was uncalled for!

Tango: Fuck you both! Liza hasn't been out of this room since last night at dinner, because she's afraid of bikers and you know why. Now imagine, a woman who is already skittish because of her situation, has some strange woman come to her door demanding things of her, in an unfamiliar place, where she doesn't know what to expect. Amy just ramped Liza's anxiety up to fifteen from on the ten out of ten scale she was already experiencing. Her first few minutes in the clubhouse involved club whores stealing shit from her. This woman hasn't eaten since last night, because she doesn't trust the people here enough to go get some goddamn food, and you two are worried about me hurting Amy's feelings with the truth? Why don't we talk about the damage she just did to someone who already fears being here with us, and for good fucking reason?

Fox: Fuck, dude.

Whiskey: Sorry, I didn't even think.

Tango: That's fuckin' obvious. Talk to Amy. She started this bullshit today, coming to Liza about a problem she thinks she has with me. Liza doesn't need Amy's made-up drama on top of her own shit. Amy also does not get Liza's details, but you better make it clear that she is to be left alone.

Whiskey: Will do. Sorry, man.

"Hey, when you're done there, I'll take you to grab some food, okay?" I called out over the sound of the shower.

"Sure, thanks."

12. THE BUNNY IN THE MIDDLE

LIZA - 2 WEEKS AGO

ONCE I WAS READY AND WEARING JEANS, A T-SHIRT, AND A HOODIE sweatshirt overtop of it so that the sleeves could hide my wrists, Tango guided me out of his room and down into the commons. "I was going to take you out to get something, but I think it's better if we stay here."

"Is it because it's too dangerous to take me out?"

"It's easier from a security standpoint, but I want you to get used to being around these guys. I don't want you starving all day if I have to go to work, babe. That shit is not cool."

I swallowed hard not knowing what to say. He had me pegged. I hadn't left the room because I wasn't comfortable doing so on my own. I didn't know biker protocol for a single woman wondering around the place. I knew some wore property patches while others were free game for anyone. I didn't want to be mistaken as free game. So, I just stayed put and tried to work.

"You'll get used to us all soon enough," Tango was saying as Rabbit bounced up to us with his undeniable energy.

"Good to see you out and about, finally," he offered with a genuine smile. If there was anyone in the clubhouse that I trusted, beyond Tango, it would be Rabbit. Despite the fact that he stood up for me earlier in the day, there was just something about him that made me feel comfortable.

"Thanks. Got hungry," I admitted which caused him to frown.

"Please, tell me you've been out of the room to eat at some point today, and I just didn't see it."

I shook my head and watched as a silent conversation seemed to pass between the two men standing with me. "Okay, you have my number now, remember? If this guy isn't here, you text me if you need something. You want an escort to get around this joint; I'll be that when Tango can't be here. Okay?"

I offered him a sweet smile of thanks, because I couldn't even begin to explain the amount of relief I felt in that moment. "Thanks, Rabbit. It seems like I keep owing you today."

"You don't owe me shit, girl. Stop saying that. I'm glad to help where I can. Now, let's get your ass to the kitchen before it loses any of that bounce you got going on back there," he teased. The growl that came from Tango didn't appear to be a joking matter, though Rabbit chuckled in response. "Calm down, buddy. Just appreciating the fine curvature." He held his hands up as he walked backwards. "I'm keeping my hands to myself, see." He grinned again and then turned to finish the walk back to the kitchen area.

"He's our resident good-time guy," Tango explained, unnecessarily. "Always in a good mood, always joking around. When it comes to doing his job, he's completely serious though. When he says you can trust him to be the person to go to when I'm not around, he means it."

"I already made that assumption when he told those other guys the truth about what went down today. I'm just glad he was there to witness it because I really don't think they would have believed me or even listened. She didn't exactly lie to them, but she wasn't forthcoming about how she approached me either, making it seem like I was a complete bitch for no reason."

"I know. I am sorry about that. I can't believe she did that shit. Amy's always been a solid person since we met her. I guess they're having a hard time understanding why she would behave differently now."

I grunted a non-committal response that made Tango stop and turn to me. "What does that mean?"

My sigh should have been all the answer he needed to understand that I didn't really want to talk about it, but he nudged me with his shoulder, so I went all in and told him.

"It's like I explained before, she's jealous and territorial. That's the difference. I'm guessing, since you said you haven't dated or whatever in a couple years, that she hasn't felt threatened by any other women before. Suddenly, I'm here, in your space, and she can't see what we do or don't get up to in private. It's killing her and that's what today was all about."

Tango remained quiet as he digested what I had to say. Before long, he grabbed my hand and pulled me along to a door that Rabbit had disappeared through moments earlier. I wouldn't push him any further where Amy's agenda was concerned, unless she stepped up to me again with fresh demands of my time or his space.

13. A SURPRISE INSIDE

LIZA - PRESENT DAY

I HAD BEEN STAYING IN THE ACES HIGH MC'S CLUBHOUSE FOR A little over two weeks and was finally starting to feel comfortable with everyone. A few of the men who had come up from Cedar Falls were still visiting Charlie, who I had since made friends with. She was a lovely woman who had been dragged through some shit thanks to a man in her life. That gave us something in common that helped us bond instantly. Since the guys from the Cedar Falls Chapter had stuck around to hang out with Charlie for a while longer, I was still sharing a room with Tango. While I wished like hell most days that it meant that we'd attempted kissing again, or more, nothing had happened. There had been a couple of nights where we'd managed to share the bed together – fully clothed – and the most that happened was us waking up tangled together before he had to rush off to work or to handle club business.

Despite the lack of intimacy, Tango and I were growing closer. We talked non-stop when we were together. We even started working side-by-side on occasion when he was frustrated with a commissioned piece he had taken on. He asked for my input on how to put a feminine spin on the original artwork, and that was all she wrote.

Our collaborative efforts ended up being an amazing three-quarter sleeve he inked on a woman who had traveled here to get the tattoo done by him specifically. Apparently, she'd seen his work at the expo, but since he left early, her appointment with him had been cancelled. It lifted my spirits immensely to work with him on the tattoo, because I hadn't been able to do that type of work since my brother's troubles started up again. I had been stuck in graphics design hell for websites and managed to make a few book covers too, but I had missed the tattoo work. Granted, I still had never actually inked a person's skin, but helping draw out the initial piece of work with Tango had been an amazing collaboration.

He and I were sitting in the kitchen with Rabbit when Amy walked in. Tango had his back to the door, but Rabbit and I were both in a position to be able to see her saunter up behind Tango and lean in seductively. It didn't seem to matter to her that the man couldn't even see the sultry looks she attempted to pull off. Rabbit hit my knee with his under the table when I didn't successfully stifle a giggle.

Amy eyed me quickly, then leaned in around Tango's shoulder and tried to plant a kiss on his lips as he turned his head to see who had invaded his space. He flinched back so quickly that her lips barely ended up grazing his jaw, leaving a line of her red lipstick trailing in their wake.

"What the fuck?" he asked as she backed up enough to have her lips close to his ear. Despite being in whisper range she spoke loud enough for us to hear her. "It's me baby. Sorry to startle you, I just came to share our good news, love."

"Baby? Love? What in the hell are you saying, Amy?"

"Why don't you come to bed, baby, and I'll remind you just what we usually do?" I snickered, causing her to turn a white-hot glare on me. "I don't know what you're laughing about. I'm his Old Lady, and you're just a job."

I continued to smile at her, because I knew the truth of their relationship. I also knew there was a major miscommunication somewhere between all the parties involved and that Tango hadn't really had a chance to address it because someone in that group was always busy over the past week and a half. The poor man wanted them all together for their talk so there would be no further misinterpretations of the situation. I understood his reasoning, but it seemed the wait was about to bite him in the ass.

Tango slid his chair back, bumping into Amy as he did so. He turned his body as he removed himself from the chair in order to stand and face her. "What in the absolute fuck is going on with you right now?" Whiskey and Fox had just entered the kitchen, too and stopped in their tracks at Tango's outburst.

"Like I was saying, I have news to share, baby. I wanted to be the one to tell you, personally. I'm ten weeks pregnant! We're going to have a baby!" She seemed so happy, even if she was delusional about who her baby daddy was. Each man around us had a different reaction from Rabbit glancing between everyone involved and me, to the other guys groaning in response, and finally to Tango who looked beyond livid at the scene the woman was causing.

"You may be pregnant, but it sure as fuck isn't my baby," he yelled at her.

"Dude, what is your problem?" Whiskey bellowed back at Tango.

"Watch how you speak to her," Fox added as he moved closer in a protective gesture.

"There's a chance," Amy pouted, hurt evident in her voice. "It could be-" she started to say, only to be cut off quickly by Tango.

"There is zero fucking chance unless you can suddenly get knocked up by guzzling jizz." Tango seethed. I flinched at the anger behind his words, even though I understood his frustration with the entire situation. "I've never fucked you. I never even put my dick anywhere near any part of your body other than your mouth. Hell, my dick hasn't been in any pussy in years, so it's fucking impossible for me to be anyone's daddy unless that kid is like six years old at this point, since I know for certain Camilla never had my baby.

"But we've..." Amy started again.

"No, we fuckin' haven't."

"You've been with us," Whiskey starts to add, a puzzled look crossing his features as he started to argue with Tango.

"Yup, and all she's ever done with my dick is suck it to take the edge off. She only got the chance to do that, because you guys kept trapping me in these uncomfortable situations that you just wouldn't fuckin' let go of. Jesus! You see where it's gotten us? This isn't fuckin' healthy! You've had me stressed out for months and trying to find ways to dodge the three of you." He pointed at the redhead then. "She's fucking delusional about shit, and you guys are still just as fuckin' clueless, because you won't hear what I've been telling you. This shit you have going on?" he questioned them as I watched in wide-eyed anticipation for what Tango was going to say next. "This is not my shit. I didn't choose this. I am not a part of your little group, other than during those few times you dragged me into the middle of things."

Fox stared, flabbergasted for a moment before he was able to speak. "You two have been together alone. Whiskey and I have left you to it, because we thought it was just being with us that made you uncomfortable."

"The only time I have ever been alone with Amy was when she needed someone to talk to. I listened and gave advice. She got enough dick between the two of you. She didn't need me giving her more, and quite frankly I was cool as fuck with that. I never wanted her that way." Tango realized the impact of his words when she whimpered, and he turned his attention back to Amy.

"You're a great girl, but this whole scenario was never anything beyond a good time once or twice, and then a few more times that I was dragged into shit. Suddenly, you're wearing a property patch that apparently includes my name – without my consent – I might add. No one fucking asked me my fucking opinion. Hell, until Liza pointed it out, I thought the "T" in that goddamn patch was just a fucked up plus sign, because there was no way you guys included me in a something as important and meaningful as a property patch without talking to me first, right?"

Whiskey was the first to respond, and it was more of a surprised exclamation than a response. "Holy fuck! How the hell did this all get so messed up?"

Fox stood there scrubbing his hands down his face and shaking his head back and forth in apparent disbelief.

Rabbit leaned over and whispered in my ear, "You need a beer? I think I need a beer for this shit storm." I managed to nod my head as he stood to go grab a couple beers out of the refrigerator behind us.

Fox turned toward Amy. "You told us you two were together when we left you alone." While there was a bit of accusation in his tone, he still did so cautiously. Clearly, he didn't want to upset her any more than she appeared to be, but he was also starting to see that maybe this woman was not quite as glued together at the seams as they thought she had been.

"Look," Tango finally managed to eke out as Rabbit handed me a bottle, and Amy purposely avoided answering Fox's accusation with an audience present. "Congrats to whichever of you is the dad. I'm excited for you, if you're all happy about this, but I'm not a part of it. If any of you had ever fuckin cared to notice, I never have been. I'm with you guys all the time, or I was, because we've been close for so fuckin long. Living, breathing, and working as a unit does that to people. You guys brought Amy into that dynamic and assumed a fuck of a lot where I was concerned. Hell, I thought my actions – or inactions – made it pretty clear where I stood. I was wrong in assuming that you guys still knew me well enough to understand where I was coming from."

Tango looked like he was ready to collapse under the weight of his strained friendships, so I stood up and moved toward him, placing my hand on his back for support. "Are you okay?" I asked the words quietly, so as not to disturb everyone else while they were mulling over everything he'd said. The man shook his head as he watched his friends, men he considered as close as brothers, process the depth of what he'd conveyed to them. Not a damn one of them had cared enough about him to see that something wasn't right in their dynamic. Not a single one bothered to see how he felt, to ask questions, or to even know how exactly he was being included or excluded in their little group activities. They were oblivious to him while thinking he was a part of their shared experience. It was sad.

Amy narrowed her eyes on me, but I stood firm with Tango anyway. Then she gave him her hurt, puppy-dog eyes. "I thought you loved me. You've said-" She started only to be cut off by the man who was having absolutely no more of her shit.

"I've said, 'love ya,' to you just as I say it to my friends." He tossed up a hand to indicate he meant all the brothers in the club, not just the two Amy was linked with. "It's the same way I'd say it to my sister, my mom, good friends even. I've never told you that I love you or that I am in love with you. There has never been a single romantic conversation between the two of us. I've never had intimate moments that could have been misconstrued beyond a friend who has, on occasion, had my dick in her mouth. I allowed myself to be trapped into those situations by guilt, and I regret that immensely right about now. Somehow, in doing so, every single one of you forgot I was a person with my own feelings, thoughts, and my own fucking life. Hell, I have never even kissed you on the mouth. Ever. Does that seem like something a man in love would avoid doing?"

Amy broke down then, crying her little heart out as if it had been broken. Never mind the awful position she had been putting Tango in all this time based solely on her own misconceptions or delusions. My bet was on delusions, considering she'd led the other men to believe that she'd been fucking Tango solo.

"Our minds are fuckin' blown right now, Brother," Fox finally said as Whiskey held onto a weeping Amy.

"Really?" Tango asked incredulously. "They shouldn't be. I've never feigned more involvement than you guys shoved at me. I never looked pleased when you tried to include me in your 'group couple talks'. Hell, I usually walked away to give you all privacy unless you sought out my personal advice on something."

"But you never said anything about the property patch when we showed you before we gave it to her," Whiskey added.

"I said, congratu-fuckin-lations. I thought the T was a plus sign. You know, belonging to Whiskey AND Fox. It wasn't until your speech that night that I realized maybe there was more to it. I figured we could have that conversation when I got back from the tattoo expo. Then shit hit the fan, and I could never get the three of you in the same place at once after I got back. Hell, it took me talking it through with Liza to realize that everyone else in the fucking club thought I was part of some weird quadro-relationship, too. It never occurred to me, because I never saw myself in it beyond friendship to each of you."

Everyone stood there staring at him for so long, I thought that was going to be the end of it. Then Whiskey spoke. "We thought we were helping you, at first, to get over Camilla. It had been so long. Then, it just seemed like you were a part of everything, and the word you're looking for is polyamorous."

"Fuck man, seriously? If I were going to claim a woman, don't you think I would have been a part of planning that shit out? No offense and carry on with whatever floats your boat and works for you guys, but when I claim a woman, it won't be as a package deal where she's shared with someone else. And I certainly won't be wondering whose baby is in my woman's belly when the time comes. The both of you should know at least that much about me considering what I went through with Camilla, and all the things I've talked to you about over the years."

Both Fox and Whiskey flinched at that speech. Whether it was because they should have known their friend better, or not knowing who the baby's dad was, I wasn't sure. It was clear to me that something had been fractured in the friendship of these men when Amy came along. Not that it was her fault at all, but they just stopped communicating properly when another person was tossed into the mix with their own ideals clogging reality.

I hurt for the man who became invisible, nothing more than a toy to be used as needed, to his very best friends. It sounded harsh, but how else could you describe their complete lack of insight?

"Maybe we should get you out of here, so everyone can process what just happened?" I finally asked as I applied a little more pressure on his back.

"Yeah, that sounds like a plan," Tango agreed as he started moving forward.

"It's all because of her," Amy cried out, pointing an accusing finger my way. "She's the reason you grew so cold. She's the reason you're trying to deny what has always been there between the four of us."

"Amy, you're emotional, pregnant, and you're going to regret saying things when you look back. T is right. None of us cared to see that he wasn't into this. Thinking back, I can see it written on his every expression. Every time he tried to ask for more jobs that took him away. All the extra time he put into the studio, even when it was all finished. It all makes sense now, and I'm so sorry we didn't see that shit sooner, Brother." Fox stated while Amy continued to wail and blubber about how it was all my fault and Fox was lying.

If that was what being pregnant did to you, I would rather not. As I was thinking that, I remembered what Michelle, my brother's girlfriend was like, and I realized that Amy was not the best example of what to expect when expecting. Despite all the strife in their lives, Michelle was the most positive, upbeat, beautiful pregnant woman I had ever seen. One day, I wanted to grow up to be a mom just like her. Also, I hoped someone smacked some sense into me if I ever behaved the way Amy just did publicly. "She probably needs some therapy," I surmised.

"No doubt," Tango huffed making me realize I must have spoken the last part out loud.

"Oh shit, sorry. I thought that was my inside voice," I told him. He stopped in his tracks on the stairs and turned to smile at me while trying to stifle a chuckle.

"Don't be sorry. Not like everyone else that heard that shit storm wasn't thinking the same fucking thing. Hell, I think I need therapy after that cluster-fuck."

I laughed with him then. "Come on, let's go draw it out, big guy!" I challenged as I shot passed him on the steps heading toward our room. "Art is our kind of therapy!"

"You're damn right it is!" he agreed as he followed behind me.

14. FRIEND-ZONED
TANGO - PRESENT DAY

I T WAS TWO HOURS LATER, AFTER LIZA HAD ME BURIED DEEP IN THE middle of a rebranding project she'd been working on for a client, that there was a knock on our door. I notice Liza cringe in response and had to agree with that sentiment. I honestly just wanted to continue getting lost in our project for a bit longer and forget that all that drama had gone down in the kitchen of the clubhouse for too many ears to hear. No doubt, the grapevine had already spread, and ramped up the drama, too.

I stood and moved over to the door, answering it while also blocking Liza from view as she was lying across the bed with her sketchpad stretched out in front of her. Her tongue was poking out the side of her mouth again, like it often did when she was concentrating. I smiled then turned back to the person at the door.

"What's up?" I asked.

"Can we come in for a minute, to talk?" Both Whiskey

and Fox were standing there looking beat all to shit emotionally.

"I'm not sure now is the best time for this," I told them. It was the truth. We had all just had a huge emotional blowup. I was sure their end was far worse than mine, since they had Amy to deal with afterward. Two hours didn't seem like enough time to process that shit before trying to address any of it.

"I get that, but it seems like we keep waiting for a right time for this conversation and it isn't happening," Fox interjected.

"Yeah, I suppose so. Where's Amy?"

"She's sleeping," Whiskey stated with a hint of aggression in his voice. Fox must have caught it too, because he popped his hand back and caught Whiskey in the gut with a warning shot.

"None of this is T's fault, dude. Keep that in mind, yeah?" Fox warned him.

"Sorry, it's just difficult to wrap my head around everything that was said, and I think Amy's right. None of this was an issue before that chick came along."

"None of this was an issue before Amy came along," I stated none too kindly. "If you'd been paying any attention to what was going on with me, instead of having your head lodged so far up Amy's ass that you couldn't see straight, you would have known exactly how I felt and where I stood with everything."

Whiskey stepped back as if I had struck him physically instead of verbally. "You're blaming Amy?"

"No, you fucking idiot. We all get a piece of blame in this shit show. The only person who doesn't get any blame is the one that you and Amy can't seem to see past. Liza isn't here because she wanted to be. She didn't ask to be air dropped right into our fucking drama, and I don't appreciate you pulling her into it.

"On that note, no, we can't fucking talk in my room, because Liza is in here, and I'll be damned if I'll allow you to go on the attack with her when she's done abso-fucking-lutely nothing to deserve it. Hell, she's been the only impartial person I've had to discuss this shit with. She's been the only one who would listen to my frustrations about how you two just kept assuming shit and pushing me in a direction that your clueless asses should have known would not have been something I was okay with. I get you thought you were trying to fix something you saw as broken in me. I

You both failed to understand that I wasn't fucking broken. I was waiting for the right person to come along who would pique my interest. That person was not Amy. Even if I didn't have to share her with the two of you, it still wouldn't have been Amy, because I don't see her like that. There's zero chemistry between us. It should have been plain as day to either of you if you cared to see what was right in front of you. Or what wasn't."

Fox held up his hands. "Look, I'd rather not have this conversation in the hallway for every asshole in the club to listen in on. If you don't want Liza to hear what we have to say, send her away somewhere. She's become buddy-buddy with Rabbit, too from what I've seen. Send her to him. Hell, she can stay and listen, for all I care. We just want a chance to talk things out with you before we end up losing a friend."

I turned my back on them but left the door open so they could enter. Liza sat up on the bed abandoning her sketchpad where it lay, next to the one I had been working in. "I'll just go, and leave you guys to it," she suggested.

"You don't have to," I told her.

"It's okay. I texted Rabbit. He's going to teach me how to mix drinks down at the bar with him and Charlie. You guys need some alone time to sort your shit, and I could use a drink." She offered up a bright, encouraging smile, patted me on the arm, and took off for the door. Before she could get it open, Fox stopped her.

"I just wanted to say that we are sorry for the way Amy treated you since you've been here. It's not been fair to you, and you shouldn't have been dragged in the middle of all our mess."

"That's all well and good, but any apology needs to come from her, and I just don't see her doing that." Liza answered him before turning and leaving the room.

"She's not wrong," Whiskey responded to the closed door.

"No, she's not," I agreed before turning to my buddies who were looking around my place like they'd never been here before. To be honest, it had definitely changed, and I couldn't help but hear that little voice in my head that said, 'it's for the better too'.

"Things look different in here," Fox finally announced, mirroring my own thoughts, and proving we still had the chance to get back to that close-knit friendship we once had where we enjoyed being on that save wavelength.

"Well, things change over time."

"Yeah, I get that, but it looks almost like a fucking home in here. You have your guy shit," he pointed to some of my clothes strewn across the loveseat. "And you have the girly shit," he added as he pointed out some of Liza's makeup sitting on the bedside table on her side of the bed. She didn't wear a lot, but she had it just in case her 'face was fucked up in the morning'. Her words, not mine. Fox pointed to the bed where Liza and I had been working before they interrupted.

"Then you have that," he stated with a wave of his arms as he stepped closer and took a glance at what each of us had been working on. "You're doing work together?" he finally asked.

"Yeah, she helped me on a tattoo consult I had last week, and now I'm helping her with a rebranding campaign she's working on." I shrugged my shoulders as if that was no big deal. Fox took the time to really examine my response. He seemed to come to some conclusion as he stepped back and crossed his arms over his chest.

He shook his head back and forth for a minute, as if he couldn't believe the words that were about to come out of his mouth. He spoke them anyway. "We haven't been there for you." It was a simple statement, but it had both Whiskey and me snapping our full attention to him. Fox turned from me to Whiskey and frowned. "We haven't. We've failed our best friend, because we were too caught up in our own shit. We didn't even help you get Liquid Lines set up."

"We offered, a few times, and he kept refusing," Whiskey protested.

"Yeah, I imagine that's because he was trying to run away from our bullshit instead of getting sucked into more of it." Fox turned back to me, as did Whiskey. "I'm not wrong, am I?"

"You're not wrong," I agreed.

"Why the fuck couldn't you talk to us about it?" he asked.

"I tried."

"The fuck you did," Whiskey argued.

"The fuck I didn't. You just wouldn't hear me. Every time I told you that the group sex wasn't my scene, you pulled me in anyway. You fucking screamed your rally cry of, "It's time to get over Camilla". I was long over my ex, but you never gave me even a second to talk about her, the fact that I was over her, or anything else. You just blew it off every time, like I was still pining away because I wasn't jumping on the nearest pussy. I knew what I fucking wanted and needed in my life, and it wasn't easy pussy to take the memories away. I wanted a fresh start with someone who wouldn't walk into a tainted past if they came here and found a dozen club whores and your girlfriend that I'd been fucking. I never wanted to bring a woman into a situation where she would have to wonder about my fidelity or what some BRAT might say when I wasn't there to hear it." I slumped into the chair that sat in the corner, ignoring Liza's clothes that were spilling off the back of it.

"I was making sure that when I found the right woman, she would be okay with my lifestyle, comfortable being around my friends and family. I wanted to make sure I deserved her as much as she deserved me. You get what I'm saying?"

"Shit," Fox breathed out in frustration as he realized the true impact their behavior had on me. "And we stole that shit from you anyway." I didn't answer as he looked around and took in the well-lived-in state of my room. "She's perfect for you, isn't she?" he finally asked.

"Yeah, she is," I agreed easily.

"And we fucked it up before she ever got here, because we were too stupid to listen to what you were actually telling us. We thought..."

"I know what you thought, Fox. I just couldn't convince either of you that you were wrong, especially when you had your girl telling you that I was just in denial the whole time. I don't know what her deal is with me, but I've explained it to her, in more ways than one, that I was ONLY her friend. There should have been no misunderstanding there." I sighed.

"Then from the moment I brought Liza here, she's been in her face about how I belong to the three of you. I fucking don't. I explained everything to Liza, so she would under-stand. I did that the first day Amy got in her face while trying to get into my room – a room she should have never felt she had the right to enter without my permission – and I thought that would be enough. You know? I thought, okay, this is all out in the open. She knows my truth, but damn it, every time we get settled, and I feel like we might be able to move forward a bit, there's another load of drama popping up. I watched her cringe, as I had to go over what kind of sex I did and didn't have with Amy while she stood there listening and watching earlier. That is not a conversation I ever hoped to have with the woman I'm falling for standing there watching."

Both Whiskey and Fox stood there looking as shell-shocked as I felt by admitting I was falling for Liza. "I shouldn't have to put off my feelings for a woman I'm sharing space with, because I'm afraid of the drama that's going to creep up on us. I shouldn't have to fucking deal with having to talk about sexual acts with another woman in front of her. I shouldn't have to deal with having a woman claiming to be pregnant, with my baby when that's damn well impossible, in front of the woman that I am falling in love with."

I tossed a pencil that attempted to lodge itself into my upper thigh and shook my head as I watched my friends react to what I'd just said. "Liza shouldn't have to deal with any of that shit at all." By the time I got that last little bit out, my voice had risen to a bark, just below a yell. There was no holding back, though. My best friends were just as culpable as their girlfriend in causing the problems that Liza and I now faced on what seemed like a daily basis.

"I blame all of you for this. I'm fucking pissed as hell at you both and at Amy too. You're all fucking ruining something that could be so fucking good for me!"

I pointed to the bed. "Look at that! Fucking look!" I yelled when Whiskey didn't seem inclined to take his eyes off me. "I've never been so at peace before in my life as I am while sitting side-by-side with her just doing our thing. Look what happens when we attempt to grab onto that peace together, though. We couldn't even have two fucking hours together, because she was trying to talk me through all the shit that just went down in the kitchen a while ago. You took a moment that should have been fucking Nirvana for me, and you spoiled it with your selfish ass bullshit."

I tugged at the lengthy spikes on the top of my hair in frustration as they both watched my every move. "I never wanted to lose either of you as a friend, I never would have thought there would come a time when I didn't have your backs and you didn't have mine. I gotta say though, I don't want any of you near me right now, because you're taking the one good thing I have had in a really long time and you are painting it with a taint so thick, that I don't know if I can dig my way back out. The one thing I was trying to avoid happening, if I ever found a woman that was worth my fucking time, and it's coming from my best friends. Not some strange club whores like I had imagined when I avoided random pussy. No, she's getting kicked out of our room so we can rehash the drama you guys and your girlfriend have brought into my life, unwanted and uninvited. You are supposed to have my six, man."

I slumped over a bit, because it literally felt like the weight of the world – at least my part of the world – had dropped right on top of my shoulders.

"I tried being her friend. I tried placating you guys even when it fucking didn't sit right with me. I tried to make everyone else happy, but when the fuck were any of you going to think about me and what I actually wanted? Now, you've fucking spoiled what I wanted. How the fuck do we carry on a friendship, when all I see is what you've ruined for me with your selfishness?"

"Jesus, man!" Whiskey finally spoke up after my voice broke on the last. "Holy fucking hell. I didn't... we were..." he glanced in desperation at Fox who looked just as lost. "How the fuck do we make this right?"

"Take Amy away from the clubhouse. You guys have a place in town. Take her there and keep her away for a while. I don't fucking want to see her after that shit she just pulled. You guys might not have known that I never had sex with her, because she led you to believe otherwise, but she damn well knew better. I am not okay with what she did today. That was purposeful and malicious, and then she tried using her tears and crying to get you to miss the fact that not only did she lie to you about the extent of our alone time, but she was knowingly starting drama in front of Liza. She purposely attempted to sabotage something that makes me happy. Whether it was just a simple friendship with Liza, or a budding relationship, it doesn't matter. Amy set out to fuck that up for me, and you two didn't just stand by and watch, you helped her. Whether you realized you were doing it or not. You want to make shit right, keep her the fuck away from me until I am ready to deal with her. Her feelings on the matter mean fuck all to me at this point."

"We will," Fox said without hesitation.

15. BACK FOR MORE
LIZA

Why don't you do those fancy bartender moves I see in movies?" I asked Rabbit as he poured another shot.

"Look around, woman! Who the fuck would I be impressing with those moves? My brothers or their Old Ladies?" He shook his head dramatically back and forth. "The BRATs want to sleep with me anyway, so I don't have to bother trying to impress them, do I?

"I suppose you have a point," I laughed as I agreed with him. "Want me to show you some tricks I learned when I worked in the casino bar?"

"Oh, hell yeah!" One of the guys sitting at the bar shouted. I wasn't familiar with him since he wasn't around often.

"Shut it, Mech!" Rabbit hissed at him, then he turned his bright smile on me. "Okay, Ms. Bartender Badass, show me your skills!"

"Be prepared," I stated, building up the tension. I took a fifth of rum, a glass, a lime wedge, and pulled the spray nozzle that the soda came out of so that it was closer to me. I popped the lime wedge in my mouth peel side first, so the wedge was facing outward. Then, I flipped the cup, started a slow pour of the rum, and took the soda spray nozzle and started spraying while I had it aimed at Rabbit. It took a full minute, and me spitting out the lime wedge as I laughed, before the other guys realized that I'd set Rabbit up. Then, they joined in, laughing until one fell off his bar stool and Rabbit came out of his shocked stupor.

"You little bitch!" he yelled as I stayed doubled over in laughter. That was until he pulled the seltzer water sprayer and began hosing me down, too. We were both laughing so hard that it took us a minute to realize we were being pelted with maraschino cherries. "What the hell?" Rabbit yelped as one nearly got him in the eye. "Damn women!" he hollered as he stood up and I glanced over to see Charlie laughing at our antics even as she helped out with a bar wars by slinging cherries at us.

"I hope you both know that you're cleaning this mess up before I go back to work behind the bar." Both she and her man, Rage, were standing there with Iceman and Rabbit's brother, Spinner, laughing their asses off.

"Guess she taught you a trick after all, huh, Brother?"

"Fucking hell. I knew not to trust a woman!" Rabbit joked as he popped me with a coiled-up hand towel that he snapped at my ass.

I started mopping up all the soda spray as I continued laughing. "Totally worth it!"

Rabbit looked at Iceman then, "I hope you know we're

keeping her around. I don't care what goes down with her brother back home. I vote that Liza gets to stay."

"Oh, me too!" Charlie seconded the motion while hopping up and down in her seat as she hit Rage in the side to make sure he knew she meant business.

"Well, you get my vote by default, because I like sex!" Rage announced, clearly not ready to go against his woman's thoughts on the matter.

"I don't know why you assholes are voting like it counts. If she wants to stick around, she can stick around. I have no problem with that. Now, get this mess cleaned up, and give me a beer while you're at it." Iceman's smirk gave him away despite his gruff demeanor. He liked me, too!

For the first time in a long time, I felt like I belonged somewhere. More importantly, I felt safe with these people. That feeling meant everything! My happy-joy-filled feelings were somewhat short lived when little miss "I'm pregnant with every man's baby" came strolling up to the bar.

She ignored the rest of the people gathered around and gave a cursory glance to the wet state of things – me being one of those things – before launching in with her request. "Can you and I talk?" I turned to glance at Rabbit who just shrugged at me, as if to say that was entirely up to me.

"Sure, why not."

"Of course, you'll talk so you can get out of cleanup," Rabbit joked. He also tapped his cell phone to let me know he was just a text away if I needed him. "Use the bar break room in back there," he said as he tipped his head to the door behind where we had been working.

"Good call," Iceman told him for some reason. I tipped

the hinged section of bar back so that Amy could get back there, and then we both walked to the little room beyond the storage area.

"What did you want?" I asked bluntly.

I hadn't expected an actual apology, and the venomous glare she threw my way let me know I wouldn't be receiving one. "I'm not sure how you've hoodwinked Tango, but I'm going to need for you to find your own room in this place. There are plenty of rooms down the hall with the BRATs now that you've had four of them fired and none have been replaced them yet."

"Where I sleep, or why I sleep there, is no concern of yours," I told her as I crossed my arms over my chest. It wasn't a defensive gesture. I was simply trying to keep myself from hitting a pregnant woman. She was making it feel like a damn near impossible task.

"It is when you're clearly having an effect on one of my men."

"You can stop right there. As if he didn't make his stance clear enough earlier, Tango isn't your man. He doesn't want to be your man. He never wanted anything more from you than friendship, and sweetheart, I hate to tell you, but your crazy bullshit has the friend-ship sailing away at this point, too. I'm not sure it will ever return."

She stepped closer, menacingly so. I kept my hands locked tight, but ready to spring into action if necessary. I didn't want to hit a pregnant woman, but I'd be damned if I didn't defend myself if one happened to attack me.

"You *WILL* stay away from him. We were all just fine before you showed up, and we'll be just fine once you and your problematic ass goes home again. I still don't know why you're here, but I refuse to lose what's mine, because you don't know your place."

Someone must have clued the guys in to the fact that Amy sought me out, because a booming voice carried over what she was saying in that instant. "Amy, you will back away from Liza, right now. You're about to lose a whole lot more than just Tango's friendship if you keep this shit up." Surprisingly, it was Fox who spoke up.

"W-w-what?" Amy sputtered as she turned around to see Whiskey, Tango, and Fox all glaring at her.

"You heard him," Whiskey intoned next. "You have already caused Tango enough trouble, and Liza too. Get over here. We're taking you to the house, and you are not to come back here without one of us escorting you, understood?"

"What? You can't do that! She... this is..." She turned so fast none of us saw it coming when the flat of her hand smacked right across my face leaving a burning redness behind in its wake. I stood there, breathing heavy, but refusing to touch her as Fox moved in quickly and snatched the angry little woman up, throwing her over his shoulder.

"I'm really sorry about that, Liza," he ground out as he hauled her ass out of the room, still shrieking about how everything was my fault.

"Holy fuck!" Whiskey yelled as he shook his head back and forth. "I honestly don't know what the fuck is wrong with that woman, but we will find out." He turned to me then. "Are you okay?" Just as he asked Tango came to me with a sandwich bag full of ice and placed it on my face.

"You okay, babe?" he asked gently. I nodded my head,

still too stunned to speak. "Come here," he said to me as he pulled out a chair, sat down, and then proceeded to pull me onto his lap. He kissed my shoulder and kept whispering over and over again how sorry he was.

"This isn't your fault," I reminded him.

"No, it's not. Fox and I should have done something long ago about this shit. You have our apologies. We'll keep Amy away. I already sent a message to Mech to remove her access to the clubhouse until we get her head on straight. She won't be allowed here anymore without one of us by her side. I'm so sorry, Liza. Truly. I don't understand what's going on with her, but I promise we'll figure it out."

I waved him off. "Go, tend to your woman. I suggest you go to her next doctor visit with her and let them know she's behaving oddly. There might be something wrong, hormonally speaking." I smiled reassuringly at him as I told him this and he just looked so taken aback by my words.

"The fact that you're concerned for her health after she hit you..." he took a breath before continuing. "I hope you know that none of this is his fault. We put this problem on his shoulders, he didn't ask for it. I hope you don't hold it against T."

"Why on Earth would I do that?" I asked in all honesty. I knew this wasn't Tango's fault. I would never hold someone's past relationships over their head anyway, but this hadn't been a relationship. It had been one, long, series of miscommunications. Whiskey smiled at me then.

"Good to know. I better get going. No doubt, Fox has his hands full."

Once everyone else was gone, I moved a little so that I

could get Tango to stop hiding out with his head dipped down behind my shoulder. When I finally got him to look me in the eye, I offered him a smile.

"I hope you know that I don't blame you. I don't think less of you because that woman is oddly obsessed with you. How could I? I told you about how the men who saw my scars turned me away even though that was a part of my past that was not my fault. I would never do that to someone else. You are an amazing man, and there's no way I am going to let someone else's actions and issues burry your greatness. You don't need to hang your head and take responsibility for her shit. Don't think for one minute that I don't know her drama is just that. Hers. It is not a reflection on you, Tango."

His arms wrapped around me tightly as he breathed out the words, "Thank you." He kissed my shoulder again. "You don't know what it means to hear that you understand."

"I do know." I reminded him as the memories of the times when I was judged by my scars filtered to the surface. I unconsciously ran a finger over one of those scars and suddenly Tango's hand was there closing over my own and squeezing slightly before he moved it out of the way and brought my arm up near his face as if he were about to kiss me there. I snatched my arm away.

"No!" The word left my mouth on an exhaled breath. Tango smiled at me.

"I was just looking, babe. I'm going to fix these for you, so that they won't keep tainting your world. You had a tattoo under this one before. Would you want the same thing?" I shook my head. "Okay, then you're going to think on it and tell me what you might want, and we're going to come up with something beautiful to put over this, because you are more than these scars."

He gave me a little squeeze that felt a whole lot like a full-body hug. "You are far more than that moment in time that they branded on your flesh. I want to change those memories for you and make something better." He leaned in and placed a sweet kiss right where my shoulder met my neck and then he sighed. "I think you're probably the only woman who could understand my situation without judging me for it. I should have known you'd have a better perspective on things than other women would."

Tango pulled the cold bag of ice away from my cheek. It was still red, no doubt, but I had a feeling it was just because of the ice now and not the smack. His fingers traced lightly over my cheek before they pulled away only to be replaced by his lips.

"So sorry you got hurt because of me, babe."

"Not your fault," I reiterated.

"Still, sorry. It shouldn't have happened."

"No, it shouldn't have, but it's done, and I'm tired of dwelling on it."

I put my fingers under his chin and lifted his face until his beautiful golden-green eyes were locked with my own. Then, I leaned forward and ghosted my lips over his. It was just a tickle, a hint of affection. Then I sucked his top lip into my mouth and licked it gently while eliciting a groan from Tango. It was about that time that he finally decided to throw caution to the wind and join in. His fingers dove into the hair at the nape of my neck, tugging my head into the position he wanted me in, and then he took my mouth with his in one of the most heated, sensual kisses I've had in my entire life. I would have stripped down right there and ridden him into oblivion if he hadn't stopped me.

"Why the fuck are you so sticky?" he asked as he pulled away from me, his hands having a hard time releasing my hair that had been doused in seltzer water before the show-down with Amy. I laughed and silently cursed Rabbit for inadvertently cockblocking me.

"Rabbit and I may have had a training incident behind the bar just before Amy showed up." I snickered out my response as I recalled some of what happened before Tango interrupted my story.

"I definitely want to hear all about that later, but right now I need to get you back to our room."

"I don't think anyone will bother us back here right now," I told him as he kissed me again.

"Nope, but I'd rather my brothers not watch our first time together." I looked around then thinking I'd see someone else in the room. There was no one. "Cameras," he stated.

"Oh! Rabbit is one smart bunny!" I laughed.

"He the one who told you to talk in here?" I nodded in answer. "Good. Now, I'll be able to hear first-hand what she had to say to you, and so will Whiskey and Fox after she attempts to lie to them again. Although, I think we caught enough of it for them to finally understand, especially since she hit you."

"Most likely," I agreed. "Now, enough about them. Let's go back to our room." That was all she wrote, because he stood, flung me over his shoulder and carried me out of the break room and through the commons area to the boisterous hoots and hollers of the many men still gathered around. This was the sexy kind of caveman Alpha display that women swooned over in the movies. It wasn't like the things that happened during my captivity with a different type of MC. There was nothing sexy about being kidnapped, starved, branded, and nearly raped. Nothing at all. I was thanking my lucky stars that my brother enlisted the help of Tango, and the guys of Aces High MC, this time. He hadn't just saved my life with that decision. He'd saved my soul and put me in the hands of people who would be able to help repair some of the damage that had been done before. I wasn't just talking about Tango's offer to cover up my scars with new tattoos either. The entire club, minus Amy, had my back and bent over backwards to make me feel welcome and part of things here.

There were secrets a plenty, but they weren't the kind that were there to hurt me. If anything, the secrets the men kept were designed to make sure the women stayed safe, and I respected the hell out of that. More importantly though, I was about to go finally be able to indulge in my favorite past time, seeing Tango naked. I'd seen him undressed all the way down to his boxers before and the sight alone had left me wanting and more than willing. It seemed as though it was finally time to unveil his package and get some relief for the relentless teasing I'd endured over the past few weeks of us sharing a room.

16. SOMETHING FOR ME
LIZA

As soon as we entered the room, Tango pushed me up against the door once it closed behind us. His big hands reached under my thighs and literally held me up while I wrapped my legs around him. His mouth captured mine; tongue plunging into my mouth and dueling with my own. The heat that built between us was about as unbelievable as the rather large bulge that was pushing against my most sensitive spot, demanding just as much of my attention as the man's mouth had.

My hands gripped well-defined shoulders, holding on, pulling him closer, and wishing I could rip the clothing off that separated our flesh. I managed to ball his shirt into my both my fists before the man took the hint and ripped it from his body for me. Mine was next, leaving me with my jean-clad legs wrapped around his waist while only a bra covered my upper half. Tango's mouth explored down my neck, over my collarbone, and eventually settled at the top of my breasts where the mounds were being pushed out of the c cups of my bra thanks to our frenzied movements.

Tango used his teeth to nip at the edge of one of the cups and pull it down, liberating my stiff nipple from its confines. I wasn't sure if it was pleasure, agony, sweet relief, or all the above when his mouth clamped down on my nipple sucking, biting, and licking the turgid peek with his very talented mouth while his hands went to work unclasping my bra behind my back.

Everything came together all at once. My bra slipped down my torso, he lifted his mouth, only long enough to swap which breast he was giving his attention to, and then he pulled the straps of my falling bra down my arms and tossed it across the room. He released my nipple with an audible pop as he brought his mouth back to meet my own. We were each working at the other's jeans, trying to unfasten them when a banging sounded in combination with the vibrations of someone pounding on the door that my bare back was leaning against. It startled us both out of our lust-induced haze.

"You have got to be fucking kidding me!" Tango called out in frustration.

"Sorry, T. Iceman sent for you. There's been a development in your situation." I didn't recognize the voice on the other side of the door, but whoever it was would be known from here on out as Captain Cock-block, because seriously, he couldn't have worse timing. The dude had quite literally just interrupted one of my fantasies come to life. At least, it had been about to come to life before we were so rudely interrupted.

"Shit!" Tango groaned against my neck. "If Iceman's calling me down, it's important, babe. I'm so sorry." Frustration rolled off me in waves as I dropped my legs and slid down Tango's hard body until I my feet found the floor again. Then I slowly moved out from under the cage his arms had me in and leaned down to pick up the shirt he'd flung off me moments ago.

"Go on," I sighed.

"Babe," he started while adjusting his still half-hard cock in his pants. "The last thing I want is to have to walk out that door right now, but I promise, we are going to finish this when I get back."

I smiled weakly at him and turned to the mess we'd left on the bed earlier when we'd been working together. "No worries. I'll be here when you're done," I agreed. Something made me wonder if I would be here much longer considering the way the man at the door had said there had been a development in my situation. My heart hurt when I thought that maybe these men were tired of hiding me, and I'd finally be turned over so the brutes that took me once before when I was younger could finish what they'd started back then.

Strong arms wrapped around me from behind, tugging my back into his front. "I mean it, Liza. We're picking this up as soon as I get back. And I don't want you to worry. I'll handle whatever has come up, and you remain safe here with me." He kissed my head, let go, and left the room after that. I heard him lock the door as well, making me smile, because he was always thoughtful of my security. I needed to remember that whenever I had doubts about anyone else.

Tango wouldn't allow them to hurt me. I knew it in the same way I knew how to take air into my lungs in order to stay alive. It was just sort of an innate thing.

17. THE WRONG CLAIM
TANGO

"This better be good," I snarled as when I walked into office where Iceman, Rage, and Spinner were waiting. One look at all their serious mugs, and I knew it was probably going to be worth them interrupting what had promised to be a damn good time with Liza.

"Sorry man, it couldn't wait." Rage grimaced as he spoke. "We all saw you haul her upstairs, trust that we would have given you time if it were an option."

I nodded. "What's going down?"

"Got word from King's Demons. Random put out a claim on your girl. He says she's his rightful property to take, since her brother took his Old Lady and ruined her."

I laughed. "Is that supposed to mean fuck-all to me?"

"Same for us, but his club is backing the claim, country-wide. Their Reno Chapter was nothing to worry about, but the national level is a lot. It also gives up a jumping off point. They have a chapter out near Boulder that we weren't aware of until they just hit us up with a request to meet."

"You're fucking serious?"

Spinner took over then. "Completely. They sent a request for us to meet up and negotiate for the girl's release from our care."

I glanced around the room, damn near in a desperate state. "I'm not handing her over to those assholes." I turned to Iceman then. "You heard what what went down when they nabbed her before. She just barely got out of there without being raped, she was branded for shit's sake, and she watched a slave girl starve herself to death, because death was more welcoming than the life those assholes offered her. Now, this asshole is claiming her as an Old Lady replacement. Fuck that!"

"Calm down," Iceman stated as he stood from his seat behind the desk. "I didn't say we were going to hand her over. We're just letting you know what the bastards have requested, and that trouble's brewing."

"Any luck tracking Frank down yet?" Ice's demeanor immediately changed as he scowled up at me.

"No, and I gotta say, I wouldn't mind a few minutes alone with him in a room for my own personal reasons."

Iceman once had a little sister who had been kidnapped by the local kiddie-creeper. He had been twelve at the time, his sister was only eight, and Iceman saw her being stuffed into the back of a car but couldn't get to her in time. His testimony had eventually led to the man being found, and ultimately to the time his vile ass served in prison before he was killed there. Iceman wasn't in time to save his little sister from all sorts of horrendous shit before she was eventually killed. It was a weight that still hung heavy on his shoulders all these years later. Every time he saw Liza's scars, I would see him shiver as if someone had just walked over his little sister's grave.

"I get that, man. Had I known her full story before we left Frank in Reno, I would have made that happen as well."

Iceman nodded. "We have eyes on his woman out there so if he comes around, we'll know and have him brought here. He doesn't get a choice anymore. With the damn King's Demons moving in closer to us, I have to wonder how they even knew she was here. With Frank in the wind the answer to that ain't looking so good."

I swallowed down my initial reaction and immediately started to put a plan together for how to deal with Liza when she heard the possible news that the KDs might have her brother. A small part of me hoped he was with them and pissing his pants each minute he was there, because he'd put his own sister in a worse position once upon a time. The other part of me knew that Liza wouldn't want that for her brother, no matter what she'd endured as a result of his stupidity. I wasn't certain what the fallout was going to be, but no matter what happened, Liza was my priority.

"We have men coming in from other chapters," Iceman cut into my thoughts. "They'll be here in the next couple days as we prep for this meetup we're supposed to have."

"Where exactly are we supposed to meet them?"

"I'm looking for a neutral location somewhere between us and them. I'll update when everything's set. Be prepared to get moving as soon as the others get here, though. I want to be first there, so we can get a real view look at the place before the KD's do."

"Probably be easier to do if you knew where 'there' was," Rabbit stated from over my shoulder. He and Shameless had come in during the briefing. The latter of the two popped him the stomach for the sarcastic remark and then ended up shaking out his hand.

"Damn, kid, you got metal plates in there?"

Rabbit's grin expanded impossibly wider. "Abs of steel, Brother."

"Fuckin' hell," Spinner announced, exasperated with his younger brother, as usual.

"Told you not to knock those workouts," Rabbit scolded as he turned a little, so we could all see his backside. "Check it out, I have buns of steel, too."

"For Christ's sake, are we done here?" Spinner asked as he headed for the office door.

"Yeah, we're done here, for now," Iceman declared before turning to me. "Tango, stick around."

I waited for the others to clear out of the space that seemed much too small only moments ago, but now seemed cavernous with the large-bodied men missing from it. "What's up, Prez?"

"What's up with this Amy situation? She gonna be a problem for the club?"

I sighed and then took the seat opposite of where Iceman sat on the other side of the desk. "I wish I could tell you, but the people to talk to would be Whisky and Fox."

"Whiskey and Fox have their heads up her ass and didn't see this shit storm brewing sooner, so I'm asking you."

"Honestly, I had my head up my own ass and didn't see this level of craziness coming either. I don't know if she was always a bit touched and we just never noticed it." I shook my head. "I wasn't around her as much as the other guys, so I can't say for sure. Maybe it's the hormones. Either way, the guys have informed her that she isn't welcome here right now and definitely not until she gets her shit together again. Mech removed her from the system, so she can't just show up at the clubhouse unannounced."

Iceman nodded. "How's Liza with all the drama that went down? I saw the video of that confrontation in the back room."

"She was just fine until I got called down here for the updates," I ground out a little harshly thinking back to how on fire she was for me upstairs only a little bit ago.

Iceman chuckled. "Sorry about that. Never thought I'd be the one cockblocking you." His chuckling subsided, and he leveled me with a serious look. "You gonna put your claim on her?"

"I am," I stated without a moment's hesitation.

"Thought as much." Iceman stood and came around the desk then. "She's in for a rough road ahead. Things aren't looking good for that brother of hers. We have eyes on the sister-n-law and are ready to pull her out and send her somewhere else, if need be. You need to be prepared for that. We can't take a pregnant woman on here, especially with the KDs bringing trouble so close to our doorstep, but that means your woman might feel inclined to go be with Michelle."

"Where are you going to send her?"

"Hopefully," he sighed and parked his ass against the desk. "Nowhere. Realistically, it's probably going to come down to sending her to Tallahassee. Crusher already agreed to it, and they're ready for her, if need be. Ready for Liza too, if that becomes a reality."

Crusher was the President of the Tallahassee Chapter, and an all-around good guy, even if his good guy persona was hidden under layers of rough edges and darker things. The Tallahassee Chapter was one of the few in our MC still involved in the gun trade. There chapter had a string of bad luck when they attempted to go legit previously, only to find out their former President was skimming money from the club. Then there was a whole fucking battle with the ruling family in their area that led the club into a decade's-long arms deal.

From what I heard, Crusher recently started working with the women of the S.H.E. MC to develop a realistic business model that the guys in Tallahassee could use to get themselves out of the gun trade now that most of them were settling down with their women and starting families.

"Shit," I growled as I thought about the possibility of Liza being sent to our chapter on the Florida panhandle. I fucking detested Florida and didn't want have to transfer chapters, but if it came down to it, I would. For her. Besides, it might be worth getting the space between myself and Whiskey and Fox's relationship with Amy.

"Crusher and I already spoke about the situation. He's willing to take you in, too."

My head whipped up instantly, and my eyes met with Iceman's crystalline ones. He was dead serious. "I can't transfer there. Whiskey and Fox are about to be dads, Amy's crazy, and I have a feeling they're going to need me around.

Besides, this is home." Fuck. I guess space wasn't what I needed, considering the words that fell from my mouth. The whole situation was confusing as fuck.

"That's a decision for you to make, Brother. I'm just letting you know that the choice is there if you need to take it."

"I appreciate that."

"All right, I do believe you left your woman waiting and wanting. Better go remedy that before she gets pissed and comes to hunt you down."

"She'd never do that," I told him.

"I know it. That's why I'm bending over backwards to make sure we have our ducks in a row for her. She's been through enough at the hands of a piece of shit MC. The least we can do is make sure she sees the other side of our world for what it is."

When I got back to the room, Liza was lying across the bed, out cold. I covered her, and then just sat and watched the woman I was falling for as she slept. She seemed at peace, unlike when she first got here and was always so on edge it took a miracle, and supreme exhaustion, to get her to pass out at night. I'd like to think the change meant that she had grown to trust me and was comfortable enough here that she knew she was safe. I didn't dare ask though, as if just putting the words out there would break the spell she was under and send her back to that restless space she'd once occupied.

18. SWARMING THE HOUSE

LIZA

Sitting at the bar watching Charlie work her magic with the big, bad biker boys of the Aces High MC was something special to witness. She had them eating out of her hand and laughing as she poured more beer and whiskey than anyone should ever consume. She was entertaining me, because when I woke this morning Tango was nowhere to be found. I wasn't sure where he'd gone, or when, since I didn't even register him coming back into the room last night.

After Tango left me in my turned-on state to go see what Iceman wanted, I helped myself out, and then fell off to sleep. It took me a couple hours to even come out of the room to look for anyone, because I was still leery about wandering around the compound – or whatever they called this massive place – on my own. The need for food finally broke my resolve and drove me down to the bar where I met Charlie.

When the door opened, and Charlie stilled while all the men around us jumped up, I knew something strange was going on. "What's happening? I asked as Charlie turned and shrugged before the man who I'd come to realize was like a surrogate father to her got up and went to greet the newcomers.

"Well, well, well, looks like the south is invading us, boy!" Shameless called out good-naturedly as he moved in to hug the first man in the lineup. The man in question had to be equal in height to Tango, at about six feet, four inches. That was where the similarities ended. This new man had silver hair and his well-trimmed beard matched, though it was interspersed with darker hairs too. His blue eyes were large, yet watchful. He was probably mid-to-late forties, but still fit as any of the younger men in the clubhouse.

"We had to come show you how it's done, Shameless!" The man drawled in what I was certain was an exaggerated southern accent.

"Who did you bring along?" Before anyone could answer, Shameless let out a surprised hoot of excitement. "Shit! This your boy? Damn, man, it has been a minute since I last saw you. Toby's all grown up now." The silver-haired man grinned with pride over at the younger version of himself as he slid to the side a bit, inadvertently giving me a better view.

"All grown up, and no need to be jealous, either. I'm sure there's plenty of pussy to go around for you old dudes," Toby stated before eyeing his dad. "You're not included in that."

The man scowled at his son. "Of course, I'm not. Not a bitch alive who could compare to your momma." The son nodded at his father, obviously liking that statement. My attention was pulled elsewhere though as a sturdy mountain of a man came ambling over to me at the bar.

"Hey there, honey. You don't look like the normal club fair they serve up around here." His statement gave me pause, and the leering look he sent my way did as well. I cringed and slipped backwards, almost falling off the stool I'd been perched on. As I caught myself before I managed to knock over the stool beside me. "Whoa, there little mouse," he called out, gentling his tone a bit as he threw his hands up in the air to show he meant no harm.

Warmth at my back, and the familiar scent of Tango's intoxicating leather and spice combination, worked to put me a little more at ease and calm my nerves. "Shit, she the house mouse your boys picked up?" The man asked.

Tango growled low in his throat causing the vibrations to rumble through his chest and into my back. "She's no mouse, and she sure as fuck ain't a BRAT either. Hands off, Van."

Van's eyes went wide at that. "Well, hell, didn't realize you'd gotten yourself an old lady." I started to protest, but Tango's words cut me off.

"Not yet, but she's mine just the same." As Tango spoke, I reached out to grab my sweatshirt off the bar where I'd placed it when I came down. I didn't like wearing it down here, because they usually kept it pretty warm in the place. Unfortunately, I also didn't like showing off my scars, so I was often in a conundrum as to what to do. Either way meant I was uncomfortable. When I went to grab my sweatshirt Van's eyes tracked the movement and he reached out faster than a serpent striking prey to grab my hand.

"Son of a..." he hissed through his teeth as he took a better look at my forearm, marked as it was. "Someone is going to pay for this!" he demanded, and I didn't understand the venom behind his words until Tango gentled my hand away from the man.

"Random will pay for that, and the other one," Tango told him causing the man to glance down at my other arm that I quickly hid behind my back.

"You have nothing to worry about from me, girl." Van turned and walked away. I wasn't sure if I'd offended him, but honestly, I didn't care. Strange men, especially those wearing kuttes, still put me on edge. It was a response I couldn't help.

"It's okay, none of these guys would ever hurt you, Liza."

"I know that you know all of them, and you think that, but I can't help..." He pulled me close to his body and turned me so that my head was resting on his chest while his arms locked around me protectively.

"I know. I understand, and so do they. You're fine. We're here for you, and before long you'll understand that this world is different from the one you were trapped in all those years ago. It's not the same. The people aren't the same. I promise, no harm will come to you here or at any of our chapters."

I nodded against his chest. Knowing that the men I had met in the Aces High MC were nothing like the King's Demons didn't stop my anxiety from spiking. It took work to even out my breathing and calm my racing heart. Another man walked up, just as I got myself settled back down. According to the patch on the front of his kutte, he was the President of another chapter, and his name was Crusher.

"You must be Liza?"

Again, I nodded my head, but I also scooted out of

Tango's embrace while keeping him secured at my back, because I couldn't do without the safety his presence provided me. "I am."

"Good to meet you, I'm the President of the Tallahassee Chapter, and that idiot who just made you uncomfortable is one of my VP, Van. I promise, he meant no harm." The man glanced over at Van who was having a somewhat heated discussion with Shameless. "I can assure you he's angrier with himself than you can imagine for approaching you that way. Van has a soft spot for women who have been taken against their will. One of his friends was also held captive for a while. She's doing better now, but I would lay down odds that Van's giving Shameless a heap of shit right now for not pointing you out immediately."

I offered a weak smile then. "I hope not. Shameless has been wonderful to me."

Crusher glanced over at Charlie behind the bar and then to Shameless. "I bet he has. He seems to be collecting surrogate daughters lately."

I turned to see Charlie blushing just a bit and smiling over at the man in question. "I better go talk my VP down from berating himself too badly."

"Please, tell him it's nothing personal, I just..." I started to explain myself, but Crusher cut me off.

"No need to explain. We know. Van just forgot himself, and who might be here, that's all. He'll get over it." With that the man walked off to go assuage his friend's ego.

"I told you they're all good guys, even the ones who seem a little rougher around the edges."

"I know," I answered quietly, and left it at that.

"Come on, I'll introduce you to the guys from Charleston and Sierra High, too."

"Sierra High?" I had never heard of that place before, so it made me curious.

"It's a little mountain town in Georgia. The town's basically built around a lake, peaceful for the most part, if you discount the fact that they have two MCs in residence there."

"Two for a small town is strange, isn't it?"

"Well, we moved in on someone else's territory, but lucky for the Aces High, the President of the S.H.E. MC happens to be the daughter of the National President of the ours."

"Wait, did you say his daughter's MC?"

Tango grinned at me. "You heard right. A few of the guys refer to them as the Bitch Brigade, but if you ask me, they're a badass MC all on their own. Those ladies managed to build something special there, from their security ventures to the clubs they run, they're extremely successful. A couple of our financially struggling chapters have had a sit-down with Angel Girl about her business model. We're hoping she can help get them on a fast-track to better avenues of income, so they don't have to rely on the shadier side of shit."

"Wow, I didn't even realize there were female MCs. That is pretty damn cool."

"They are few and far between, and there's more female or coed style riding clubs than actual MCs, but Jamie grew up in the club life, so I guess she didn't want to half-ass it."

"Jamie?"

"Jamie Murdock, otherwise known as Angel Girl, the Sierra High Evermore Club President."

"Oh, okay. I wish she was here. I think it'd be cool to meet her."

"I'm sure you'll meet her, eventually. We all do a charity run together down in Cedar Falls, West Virginia once a year to raise money for several children's charities. Some of the girls have promised to come up for it this year." We stopped in front of four men, including the silver-haired man and his son Toby, whose kutte indicated that he was called T-Bone. I had to work at not rolling my eyes about that one. I could only imagine how he'd earned it.

"Guys, this is Liza," Tango started the introductions. "Liza, this is Double-D, T-Bone, Grim, and Snake. Grim and Snake are from Sierra High while Double-D and T-Bone are from Charleston. You already met Crusher and Van from Tallahassee."

"Nice to meet you all," I stated while glancing between the four men.

Most of them bobbed their head in greeting, but Double-D spoke up. "You and your brother have any other family out there aside from one another?"

I shook my head. "No, both of our parents are gone now. It's just Frank, me, and then his fiancé and their baby that's on the way."

"Ever been to the Georgia Mountains before?" The one named Snake asked.

"No. The furthest east I've ever been, before coming here, was to Salt Lake City."

"Seriously?" A wide-eyed Snake asked me, his tone one of disbelief.

"Yeah, I just never had the mind to travel. I had my business in Reno and didn't really need to go much further for anything. My brother would never take me with him to conventions or expos too far from home. I think he was worried someone would snatch me up, and I wouldn't come back to help out in his shop."

"You a tattoo artist, too?" Grim asked.

"No," I stated a little too quickly. Grim was an intimidating figure standing at about six feet, five inches with black hair and nearly black eyes to match. His name fit him perfectly. All he was missing was a scythe to carry around, and people would mistake him for Death.

"I'm an artist. I usually design ad campaigns and websites and things for people. I've recently dabbled in book cover design for a few authors I met online, and I'll probably start doing a little more of that since I'm here and don't know anyone local I can get set up with."

Snake smiled brightly at me then. "My friend Poppy does the same stuff. I don't think she's ever done books though."

"Oh, you should give her my number, maybe we could network together and throw each other work if one of us has too much going on," I suggested.

"I will do that." He glanced over toward the bar, seeing that the BRATs were out and about, and that was all she wrote. "I'll get that information later, Brother," he told Tango and then he was off to the races so to speak.

"Damn, didn't take him long."

"Probably the mention of Poppy. I think he needs to wash her out of his system." The distaste in Grim's words was evident.

"You don't like her?"

"I like *her* just fine, but she is married to another brother of ours. Walker is Snake's best friend. They were both interested in her, but Walker got there first."

"That must be awkward for Snake," I mumbled.

Grim huffed out a humorless laugh. "The fool waited too long. Damn shame because I think they would have been better together than Walker and Poppy are." He tipped his head toward Snake. "Looks like he found someone to drown his sorrows in, though."

A quick glance was all it took to tell me I didn't want to turn fully in his direction. He was already making out with one of the BRATs. I'd forgotten her name, but I didn't think I'd forget the fact that both of her breasts were completely tattooed aside from her areola and nipples. It was almost like the tattoo formed a tube top on her since it wrapped all the way around, and the girl didn't see the point in wearing a shirt because of it.

"My daughter is a tattoo artist," Double-D told me, pulling my attention back to the men who were still grouped around us.

"Wow, really?"

The old man beamed down at me, and then took his shirt off really quick to show me something. "She did this," he stated, and while I could hear the pride in his voice, I felt sadness underlying that pride somehow.

I reached up and traced my fingers over the little lion cub that looked to be left behind by its family. "This is exquisite, but my heart hurts looking at it."

The man snuffled back an odd cough, almost like he was

clearing his throat of emotion. "That's exactly how it's supposed to make you fell, darlin'."

I didn't ask any further questions, because he didn't seem to want to offer any more information up about the piece. "She's obviously very talented."

"That she is," Double-D stated then turned to Tango. "You should get her up here to help out during Sturgis."

"If she'll come up, I'd be glad to have her."

"She'll be up. Her Old Man is in the club, too." I saw Tango raise a brow at that, and Double-D chuckled. "I approved. Not that either of them would have listened if I hadn't, but still, couldn't have a better man for my girl. Merc's oldest," he clarified, so Tango would know who he was talking about.

My stomach clenched a little knowing that I would never get my father's approval for Tango. If my dad were still around, I'm not sure he'd give it anyway. He had been a simple blue-collar worker, grinding out each day on construction sites wherever he could get a job. Even still, I'm not sure what he would think of the biker I found myself living with now, especially after what happened to me when I was younger. He would, no doubt, think I was nuts.

"You okay?" Tango whispered in my ear bringing me back to the conversation that was going on around me. A couple of the men were watching me wearily.

"Yeah, sorry, just lost in thought for a moment." I turned a smile on for the guys to reassure them that I was indeed fine. "I'm a bit tired. It's been a long day already. I think I'm going to go take a nap."

"Come on, I'll walk you up."

"If you're smart, you won't come back down any time soon, T," T-Bone called out.

Tango flipped him off with the hand he had tucked around my shoulder and then proceeded to walk me upstairs to our room – his room – where he shut us both inside.

"You don't have to stay with me. All your club brothers just got to town. I'm sure you want to go catch up."

"I've been catching up with them all morning. That's where I went earlier, to go with Iceman and Rabbit to give them all a tour of my shop and then to Renegade Rosy's to show Crusher and Van how we run shit there."

"Oh, that's cool," I told him. "I wondered where you'd gone this morning, but honestly, I passed out so hard last night, I didn't even know if you'd made it back there at all."

"I was with you all night. By the way, you drool a little bit in your sleep. The pillow had a puddle mark and everything." My cheeks flamed with heat as I stared at him, wondering what kind of an ass I'd made of myself in my sleep. It would be just my luck that he'd catch me drooling and probably sleep farting, too. I shivered off that thought while Tango laughed.

"Don't worry, I promise it was all very adorable. Some might say it was sexy even, especially when you rolled over smacking your lips and spreading the trail of drool as you moved."

I groaned and tossed my weary body back on the bed before giving the pillow a dubious look and moving away. That made Tango laugh even harder as he joined me on the bed and pulled me into his body. "I may only be teasing." His words were whispered into my ear right before he nipped at my earlobe and then started tickling me in that sweet spot just under my ribs where everything seemed to be a thousand times more sensitive.

"Noooo!" I cried out as his fingers dug in and found their mark causing me to squirm around and bump into various places of his body with different parts of mine. My pleading did not stop him. I shouted again when I thought I might piss my pants from laughter. "Must. Stop."

Finally, he stopped with his body on top of mine, holding most of his weight up with his arms and legs as he moved over me and stared down into my eyes before leaning in and planting his lips on my own. At first, the kiss just simmered there as our lips fused together. The minute I parted my lips, Tango pressed the advantage and slipped his tongue into my mouth. He groaned at the first taste of me, just as I returned the favor when he pulled away enough to suck my already plump bottom lip in between his own.

"Liza," his voice was raw with desire as he spoke my name as if it were a plea of his own.

"T, I want you," I told him before taking his lip and sucking on it as he'd done to mine only moments ago. That was all it took. Within minutes, he had me out of every stitch of clothing I'd put on that morning. Then he was moving to take his clothes off to even the playing field. I sat back and watched. When he realized I appreciate the view, his movements slowed, and he turned getting undressed into a sensual strip tease.

He gripped that bottom lip of his in between his teeth as he slid the zipper of his pants down and then he got up on his knees and made a production about the unveiling of his thick and veiny cock. The head of which stuck out above where he'd pulled his jeans down, thicker than the rest of him, and looking for the entire world like it would hit every sensitive spot inside my wanton body.

"I can't," he finally stated forcing me to look up and meet his eyes. His were hooded with lust and strain. "I can't be patient, baby. I need you."

"Then take me, I'm yours." In any other situation, I would have rolled my eyes at the cheesy line I muttered. Unfortunately for my idiotic sensibilities, there was no other way to phrase it. I was his. I had known it for a while, and finally telling him felt natural.

His clothes joined mine on the floor of the bedroom before he crawled right up my body settling himself in the cradle formed by my spread legs. I loved the feel of his weight draped across me as the warmth from his body seeped into mine, almost its own kind of embrace. Tango leaned in and took my lips with his once more, before blowing me away with his admission.

"I haven't kissed a woman in almost three years, and I have to say it was worth the wait."

"What?" My single word questioning response was one of shock and disbelief.

"I haven't kissed a woman since..."

"I thought you were just exaggerating when you told Amy that you had never kissed her." I shook the thought of Amy out of my head. That woman had caused enough problems for Tango and me. She attempted to cause them. Still, I didn't want to invite her memory into bed with us. "Never mind all that, come here," I all but growled before I pulled Tango closer and took another kiss from his pliant lips.

His erection rested against my pubic bone, enticing me, so I lifted my hips and rubbed myself against him like the wanton little slut I suddenly became. Pure, heated desire pumped through my veins as I took charge. I was cleanly shaven down there, which for me meant that my bush was trimmed close and everything lower was shaved smooth. The dripping lubrication before my legs made it easy for Tango's cock to slide between my lips. The movement caused another groan to fall from his lips just before he dipped his head and started to nip at my neck.

"Jesus, just this feels so damn good, babe. Dry humping like a couple kids shouldn't feel this fuckin' good."

"I wouldn't exactly call it dry," I teased causing him to laugh and wrap his arms around me to pull me over on top of him, where he immediately smacked my ass.

"Smart ass, now you get to do all the work." The smirk on his face told me he didn't plan on letting me have control long, and I wasn't stupid. By putting me in this position he was still calling the shots. It was good to see I hadn't been wrong about what I thought he'd be like in bed. And yes, I'd thought it about often. The real thing was a far better option, and one I planned to explore until I was too tired to move.

I slipped down over his hard cock and threw my head back, overwhelmed at how full I felt with him stretching me as I slid down him with a swivel of my hips. "Fuck," he hissed between clenched teeth while holding onto my hips in a grip that made me feel like he was afraid I would run. There was no way I was running from this or from him. No way in hell.

With a little encouragement from Tango, I started moving on him, lifting and plunging with little flourishes of movement thrown in to ensure he was hitting the right spots inside me. When I tilted my hips a certain way, Tango's grip tightened even more, and his panting breaths came faster and heavier than before.

I rolled my hips and dipped back down taking his full length inside me when Tango's tight control finally broke. He flipped us, putting me on my hands and knees as he entered me from behind with zero hesitation. The man went to work running one arm up under me to play with my stiff nipples and the other down around my waste to curl his fingers toward my clit and rub there.

"Fuck, Liza, I don't think I can hold out much longer. It's been so long, and you feel like heaven." A hissed breath followed that statement, as I slammed my body back into his even harder.

"Almost," I started to say when Tango's fingers got even busier on my clit; rubbing me to the same rhythm he was pumping me with. I had just been teetering on the edge when he leaned in, bit my shoulder, pinched my clit hard between his fingers, and slammed into me all at once, bringing a rushing torrent of pleasure streaming through my body. Everything between my legs was a slick mess of clenching sex. Tango pulled out at the last minute and shot his load all over my backside, taking the time to rub it in to my ass cheeks as he did so.

"I'm claiming you, babe. I need you to know that. Need you to understand. You're mine. Even if we kill them all tomorrow and leave nothing behind that could ever harm you again, I want you to stay. I want you to be here with me."

"There's nowhere else I'd rather be," I admitted before I collapsed fully on top of the bed with a good portion of Tango's weight riding down with me. My body was a tingly mass of goo. In that moment, I could have sworn I had gone completely boneless. Aside from the physical, my world had also boiled down to a peaceful, fulfilled place where Tango made me exceedingly happy and safe. Even though we hadn't said the words to one another, I also felt incredibly loved.

19. HOME ALONE
LIZA

T<small>ANGO, AND MANY OF THE OTHER MEN, PACKED UP AND RODE OUT</small> early in the morning before the sun even came up. I had anticipated the group taking me with them, but to my surprise, the subject was never even broached. I couldn't help thinking that my family's mess was the only reason they had to ride out at all, let alone en masse the way they had. I worried, and when I glanced around the commons and saw the serious faces on the few men who were left behind, the worse the feeling in the pit of my stomach grew. This was all my doing. Well, not mine, but my brother's. That was basically the same thing.

"Are you doin' all right, Liza?" Rage asked me in that gruff voice of his. I nodded my head, but he obviously didn't believe me. Instead, he patted the stool next to him at the bar. "Come on, have a seat. Charlie will be back in just a minute, and she's gonna need the company while I'm busy with other stuff today."

"I'm worried," I finally admitted after a few moments of silence passed between us.

"I know you are, sweetheart. That's normal. You shouldn't be though, because my boys won't let anything happen to T."

"I'm not just worried for Tango," I explained as I turned to look Rage in the eye. "I'm worried for all of them. This is my fucking family's drama, and your guys are out there putting their damn necks on the chopping block." My hands were flying as I spoke, as if the movement would get my point across about how serious this was.

The smile that passed over Rage's lips was genuine as he spoke. "Trust me when I say, they've got this, and not a single man isn't exactly where he wants to be right now. Those guys are there because you're ours now, too. You belong to this family as much as you belonged to the family you and your brother grew up in. He fucked up, it affected you, that means it affects us now too, and we fix it."

My lower lip quivered a bit at his proclamation. It had been a while since I felt like I was truly part of a family. My own had been dysfunctional, at best. That was even before everything that happened when I was nineteen, and my brother's craziness screwed me over. My relationship with him had been damaged irreparably back then, and it wasn't much stronger now that he's put me back in the King's Demon's crosshairs.

"Thanks," I managed to mutter to Rage as Charlie wandered up and planted herself behind the bar.

"What the hell are you doing, woman?"

"I'm going to get Liza drunk, because she looks like she needs it."

"It's not even noon," Rage insisted.

Charlie narrowed her eyes on him. "Are you telling me that with the amount of day-drinking that goes on here we can't give Liza a couple shots before noon? Are you, of all people, telling someone they shouldn't partake in the drinking before noon tradition this club was founded on?" Her questions were said in a teasing way, and his answering smirk acknowledged the fact.

Dammit, Rage, she's worried about the club brothers, for herself, her family, and her uncertain future. I know this, because it's exactly how I felt not that long ago when my own shit was going down."

I gulped down a ball of emotions, as Rage seemed to take in what she was saying. "Fine, but not too much. I don't want either of you leaving this space. I have to do some shit in the office, but Ashton and Cricket will be out here with you two, for the time being. If you need anything, just tell them, and they'll make it happen." Charlie's eyes lit up, and she started rubbing her palms together as if she had just the greedy little demand lined up for such an occasion.

"Within reason, babe."

Her bottom lip poked out in a mock pout. "You're no fun!"

Rage leaned in across the bar and planted a searing hot kiss on his woman's mouth and then winked at her as he walked away. "I'm plenty of fun, sweet cheeks, now just isn't the time for the kind of fun you like. Later though!" The promise was thick in his voice as he slid out of sight

"You better believe it," Charlie yelled after his retreating form.

"You two are hilarious," I stated as Charlie set a glass down in front of me and then lifted a finger up to her chin as if it would help her think.

"We should probably start off with something that has juice of some kind in it. That way you can say you had a healthy lunch."

I shook my head and laughed at the woman as she made me a fruity concoction that included way more rum than juice. She was doing what she set out to do. My mind was officially taken off all the things I couldn't control as I sipped the drink Charlie made for me. It was quite tasty, and after another, I was finally able to relax and let loose a little.

After three drinks, Charlie ended up ducking into the back room with Rage for a bit. Clearly, he had been ready for some of that fun he teased her about earlier. Sherry-Baby sat down beside me and smiled warmly.

"You're good for him, you know?"

"I'm sorry?" I asked, not quite understanding what she was getting at.

"Tango, you're good for him. He's smiled more lately than I've ever seen before. He's been more available to the club members since you came around, too. I think he avoided everyone before, because psycho Amy wanted everyone to think he belonged to her just as much as Whiskey and Fox did. It made him miserable a long while."

"Yeah, I gathered that much for myself."

"He's not miserable anymore. It's almost like he has this

glow now that wasn't there before. Don't get me wrong, Amy wasn't the reason he was miserable. He was all broody and no smiles before she came along. When you showed up, all that changed." Sherry-Baby nodded her head as if deciding something. "I like that about you. Tango is a good guy and he deserves someone who makes him light up the way you do."

"Well, thank you, I hope I can continue to make him happy." I took a sip of my drink and eyed the woman again. Her blonde hair curled beautifully over her shoulders, and while she wore a lot more makeup on a normal day than I would on a special night out, it was obvious she was just as naturally beautiful underneath.

"Do you have a favorite?" I found myself asking, and the question caused Sherry to blush profusely.

"I don't think I'm supposed to," she finally admitted, albeit reluctantly.

"It's just the two of us here." I leaned in closer to her and whispered, "I won't tell anyone, promise."

She giggled. "Well, I've always sort of had a thing for Rabbit. I used to crush on Steel, but he transferred to the Sierra High Chapter."

"Do you think Rabbit knows?"

She shook her head and took a sip of her drink. "No, he doesn't notice me, or any of the other girls, for that matter. He talks big about hooking up all the time, but if he does it, it's almost never here, and almost always with a girl who isn't sticking around." Her lengthy sigh dropped her shoulders instead of release tension.

"I think he has a thing for Cherry's sister. Cherry and

Chastity work over at Rosy's as dancers. It's hard to beat that twin act they do whenever Chastity shows up. That girl is pure trouble though, and not the good kind. I don't know what Rabbit sees in her, but it's a whole lot more than he's ever seen in me."

"Is he mean to you?" I was just buzzed enough that I was about to defend this girl to the man himself, if only I could conjure him out of thin air. I may have had a brief, shitty run-in with the BRATs when I first got to the clubhouse, but Sherry-Baby had never been anything but sweet to me.

"No, nothing like that. It's more like I'm invisible to him now."

"Now?"

"We were together once before, I had one wild night with him, and then the next day, when he looked like he was headed towards me for more than just breakfast, another brother cornered me. I had to watch as Rabbit walked away without another word. He never touched me again after that."

"Well, that sucks," I stated, my words the tiniest bit slurred.

She shrugged off that sentiment as Rage and Charlie reappeared from the backroom looking rumpled and wearing shit eating grins on both of their faces. "What's going on, ladies?"

"Rage," Sherry-Baby acknowledged him. She said nothing to Charlie though, and I wasn't sure if it was a deliberate snub, or if she didn't think Charlie wanted to hear from her. Either way, I figured that was their dynamic to work out.

Before I could people watch, and see how that situation

played out, my cell phone rang in my pocket. I pulled it out to see Michelle's name. I'd been given the go-ahead to communicate with my soon-to-be sister-in-law a couple weeks ago, since the club had someone keeping an eye on her.

"Michelle? What's going on?"

I listened as she freaked out, screaming and yelling into the phone, sometimes slipping into Spanish, then back to English again. I got the gist of what she was saying though. My brother had been missing for days. She thought he'd been with her cousin Lou, but Lou came around to see why Frankie never showed, and it quickly became evident that something was wrong.

"When is the last time you saw him?" I finally managed to ask, wondering if my brother was dead or alive had just sobered my ass right the hell up.

"Put it on speaker," Rage demanded as he strolled up beside me attempting to look nonchalant. I knew better. Tension rested heavy on his frame as he stood stock-still waiting for me to do as I was told. I didn't hesitate to follow his orders. The club was protecting me, the least I could do was help them out by letting them know our enemies might have captured or killed my brother.

Rage listened while tapping away on his own cell phone. He gave no clues as to who he was relaying messages to, and that didn't seem like it would change if I asked, so I kept my mouth shut.

"Michelle, this is Rage, Vice President of the Aces High MC Dakotas Chapter, there will be a man knocking on your door in two minutes. He is a friend of ours and will help you gather your things, so we can get you somewhere safe," Rage informed her.

Michelle immediately started wailing. "Oh my God, he's dead. I knew it. How am I going to explain this to our baby?"

"Michelle, you need to calm down. No one said Frankie was dead. We just want to get you somewhere you can be protected, okay?"

"Yeah," she managed to blubber out the word just as we heard a distinctive knocking on her front door. She shrieked, and no doubt jumped at the sound. Still, she asked. "Is that your man?"

"Yeah, that's our guy," Rage confirmed after checking his phone. "Go let him in."

"Okay, are you bringing me to Liza?"

"No," Rage told her as he looked at me, his eyes full of warning. It was obvious he didn't want me protesting for some reason, so I stayed quiet and listened. "It's too dangerous to have you both in the same place. It makes us a bigger target. We're sending you somewhere else, but you won't know where you're going until we get you there. That's a precaution to keep you safe, because you don't know who you can trust right now, Michelle. You get me?"

"I understand."

I understood too, but I didn't necessarily like it. I had hoped to see Michelle, so I could keep her calm. The last thing she needed was to lose her baby because of all this drama her ex-boyfriend created. Once Rage got Michelle talked down, and his buddy in the door at Michelle's place helping her pack, he called one of the guys that had gone to Casper, Wyoming.

From what I gathered, that had been the best mid-point between the Aces High MC clubhouse and the one owned and run by the King's Demons in Boulder, Colorado. It was where Tango had gone earlier, and now I wondered if my brother was there as well, or if we would ever find out that something far worse happened to him than being kidnapped and taken to Boulder as a ploy to get what they wanted.

20. IN THE MOOD
TANGO

We rode hard to get to the meetup point with enough time to set up and be prepared for the King's Demons could. A quick shot of adrenaline to the system when someone was there waiting on us, gave me the boost that I needed to chase away the exhaustion eating at my bones. A lone figure stood next to the Harley Road King Special that sat out front. I almost laughed, because it was always the older guys with the touring bikes. The man who stood next to it couldn't have been more than mid-thirties.

We maneuvered our bikes into two groups. One group posted up alongside the building and the other around the back under a canopied area that would hide them and make it look like we showed with a far fewer men. I stayed with Iceman and Shameless as we moved to greet the stranger among us, the one wearing a King's Demons kutte.

"Guy," Iceman greeted, as if this were an expected outcome.

"Iceman," Guy returned before blowing out a breath and

shaking his head. "Checked into some things. Seems you were on the level with the information you gave us. My men know the deal. They won't engage to help or hinder."

"Good to know," Iceman stated. "You know if they have Frank Rossi?"

He tipped his head down and up again as we watched. "Alive, last I saw, but worked over really well. He should be rolling in with them in about an hour. We should get some things worked out before then." Iceman agreed and moved to head into the abandoned service station with most of the other men. Shameless held me back for a minute, looking me over and noting that my whole body seemed to be shaking with pent up anger.

"What in the fuck is going on?"

"Figured you needed some explanation, so let's get this out of the way, and then you're going to do your part today."

"Which is?"

"Being a brother and doing what's asked of you. Ice has been in touch with Guy for a couple days now. King's Demons don't exactly operate in the legal realm, but they also don't traffic women on a national level. That was apparently something specific to their Reno Chapter, and while they had heard rumblings about it, no one could ever verify anything."

"Until Liza," I stated coolly.

"Until Liza," Shameless agreed. "Frank was also instrumental. Seems when they were beating him, he told them they'd never get his sister again, she wouldn't become one of their slaves like the women she saw when they had taken her before. He spouted off about the brands those assholes put on her arms. That's when Guy reached out to Iceman for confirmation. He sent pictures of your woman's arms.

"How the fuck did he get those?"

"Cameras in the bar's back room are pretty sweet, T. She was on camera in there with Amy remember?"

I remembered. It hadn't been that long ago. Shit. "Okay, so then what? You mean to tell me that the Colorado Chapter of King's Demons is about to turn on their Reno brothers?"

"That's exactly what I'm telling you. They're cutting out the bad seed."

"And using us to do it?"

"Let's say they're giving us an opportunity for some retribution before it's too late."

"Vanquish and Random both going to be here?"

"Far as I know, yeah. Random thinks he's getting the girl back, and he doesn't go anywhere without his right-hand man."

"Good. They're mine," I declared.

"Figured you'd say something like that." Shameless slapped me on the back and then walked toward the convenience store part of the old service station. "You may only get a shot at one, so figure out which one you want your vengeance on the most. Are you going to take out the one who nearly raped her or the one that put the brands on her body and gave the order for her to be snatched up in the first place?"

"Fuck," I growled. "Random then. He's the one who ordered it and the one who branded her." I could see it in my mind. I knew exactly what I wanted to do to that bastard, and it was likely going to a take damn good while before I got bored with him. I wasn't certain the guys would let me go that dark, but I was damn sure planning to make the asshole hurt before I sent him on his way to hell where he belonged.

"All right, come on, let's go find out what the plan of the day is then," Shameless tossed the words over his shoulder as if he were contemplating the daily special at a restaurant. I had to respect the man for maintaining his cool in any situation. That was why he was the club enforcer still even though he was getting older.

We went into the building, listened to the plan, and then we had to wait another forty-five minutes before the rumble of Harley engines echoed from somewhere off in the distance. From the sounds of it, there were a lot of them, too. We had been expecting at least seven from the Reno Chapter and another eight who were coming from the Boulder Chapter. Guy had let us know that ahead of time. His men would all be wearing a green armband. I tuned out what that shit was supposed to symbolize, but whatever the case, it meant that the Reno assholes wouldn't be wearing them.

They rolled up with a cocky confidence that made me wonder, briefly, if Iceman had fallen into a trap with the President of the Boulder Chapter. Guy stepped out of the building and stood beside Iceman as the King's Demons rolled up and stopped in the parking lot opposite where half our bikes had been parked. It had been imperative that the men didn't know how deep we'd rolled in, and while they were counting our bikes, I wondered if Guy had informed them before they got there. Trust wasn't my strong suit, especially where it concerned my club brothers' or my woman's safety.

"What's all this?" Random questioned while staring Guy down in some creepy big-man competition that he could never win. "The fuck are you doing here with them?"

"I'm here with them to make sure you assholes weren't ambushed," Guy stated without a hint of emotion in his voice. "You just rolled up here like you already won a fight without staking the place out first."

"I have a plan," Random laughed off the obvious disrespect from his club brother. "Right there," he added, pointing to an old rusty brown '69 Buick Skylark that made its way slowly into the parking lot. Once the car was parked, Random raised his hand and waved the occupants of the car over. Vanquish and another man got out and pulled a body from the back seat.

"Where's the girl?" Random finally questioned as his buddies dragged the limp form over to us and tossed him on the ground.

"We're not negotiating for the girl," Iceman explained coolly.

"I'm here for the girl. That was the whole point of this little powwow. This fuckwit isn't doing anything for me. The girl is mine by rights."

"The girl is mine," I stated flatly, speaking up for the first time.

Random sneered at me. "You can't claim what's mine, and I already put my marks on her. How do you like seeing my marks every time she's naked? You like knowing I did that? I branded her. She's mine."

"Seems you marked someone else who ended up claimed by another man," I antagonized the asshole. "Seems to be a problem for you, Random. What's the matter? You can't keep a willing woman by your side, so you have to take them against their will?" My glare moved from Random to Vanquish and back again. "Liza is my woman, and the last thing you'll ever do is set eyes on her again, let alone any other part of you."

"Ah, so little miss Liza's been telling stories then?"

It was obvious the beaten-to-a-pulp body at Vanquish's feet was that of Frankie Rossi. He didn't look that great, but I had no doubt he'd survive if all went well. The broken man nodded to me, and then closed his eyes, as if waiting for the inevitable to happen. It put me even further on edge, as he seemed to resigned with his impending fate.

"As I already said, we're not here to negotiate with you about the girl. She's off limits to you." Iceman's voice was cold and hard as he spoke. Random laughed, but I could have sworn I saw Frank's lips quirk up in a tiny ghost of a smile. It was a peaceful look until it wasn't.

In the next second, another man, younger than Random and Vanquish by at least ten years, moved forward and pulled a gun on Frank. With no hesitation, he pulled the trigger and plastered Frank's brains all over the parking lot in front of us. His body slumped forward with the impact and one lifeless eye stared up at me. Sickness swirled in my gut. It wasn't the dead body that did it. It wasn't that I had known Frank for years, even if we hadn't been close. The bigger reason for that feeling was knowing I'd have to tell Liza that we weren't able to stop her brother from being killed.

"What the fuck?" More than a few voices shouted.

Vanquish took the kid down to the ground and made brought him face-to-face with the corpse he'd just created.

"Who the fuck ordered that hit?" Guy shouted, and then turned to Random. "You can't even keep your own men in check?"

"Fuck," Random spit out. "Little shit's my brother by blood."

"Little shit just cost you," Guy stated and then he too pulled his gun, and the trigger, with not a single moment of thought. Random dropped right in front of us, and rage soared through me at being denied the vengeance I needed. Before I could blink, Guy downed Vanquish, too. Both men were taken out right before my eyes, but not by my own hands.

We stood and watched as Guy's men took out the rest of Random's crew before he turned to us. "I know you wanted your vengeance. You got it by bearing witness. Our business with you is done here. The women are no concern of ours. We'll clean up our own mess, including the one the rest of our club made in Reno today."

Guy dismissed our club that quickly, and I honestly didn't know what the hell to do with my anger. I wanted to put my fist straight through Guy's face, and it must have shown because he simply stood there, as if waiting for it, before Shameless took hold of my arm and pulled me away from the man.

"Let it go," he rumbled gruffly. "We need to get Liza's brother back to her."

We ended renting a small U-Haul truck to transport my bike and Frankie's body back to the clubhouse. Once everything was secured, I followed my club brothers back to Spearfish. The whole way there, I wondered how in the hell I was supposed to break the news to Liza. Sure, she was angry with her brother about the position he'd put her in twice. Despite his dumb shit, the man was still her brother. I could see it in the way she spoke about him. She loved him even though he was a fuck up. That's probably what I would have to tell her. Frankie hadn't fucked up in the end. He wanted to trade his life for hers even though that would mean he never got to see his kid born. He died for his sister, and he did it gladly. Maybe that wouldn't be a comfort for her just yet. Later, when the pain of his loss was less, it would mean something to her.

21. THE DELIVERY

LIZA

It was nearing ten that night when Rage finally reemerged from the office that he'd holed himself away in most of the day. Despite still being ruggedly handsome, Rage's appearance spoke of a hard day and even worse news to come. He glanced up at me and I saw it in his eyes. Something happened that would have an impact on me. When he didn't approach directly, and I was left to sit in the corner of the sofa I'd parked my ass on earlier, I knew that someone else was meant to deliver the news.

It made me wonder if they were going to turn me over to the King's Demons after all. I wondered if Michelle made it to wherever they were taking her to safety. Maybe the bad news was that she didn't make it. Then again, my brother had been missing. It could be that they found out he hadn't made it either. Tango flashed in my mind, and I shivered at the thought that I might have lost him before we ever truly got started. It felt like there was a two-ton damn weight on my chest making it hard to breathe.

I watched as Rage pulled Charlie into a quiet corner and spoke to her in hushed tones. I knew she had been privy to far more of what was going on than I had. There was no doubt that she would keep that information to herself, and not share with me. I didn't hold it against her, because I could see it in her eyes that she wanted to.

I might not have been around the club all that long, but I had seen enough to know that some people were privy to things while others weren't, and those were the breaks. You either lived with it, or you got the hell out of the life, because it wouldn't be for you. I knew this, and never had it felt like a true burden until that day. The hours of waiting made the lack of information feel like some sort of punishment.

I caught both Rage and Charlie as they glanced in my direction a few times before they went back to their quiet, yet seemingly heated, argument. I'd like to think Charlie was on my side and telling her man that I should be informed of what was going on. They didn't appear to come to agreement though, so I figured that no matter what, Rage would win in a battle of wills between the two.

I didn't have to wait and wonder, because only moments later, when I contemplated busting in on the conversation Rage was having with Charlie, the front door snicked open with its usual hiss and a beep that signaled the security protocol had been followed and the entrant was allowed to be admitted.

Iceman came through looking travel-worn and burdened by whatever had transpired. He noticed Rage who stood in greeting, and the two of them disappeared down the hall and into the office once more without a backward glance. Charlie also stood, but she headed in my direction with a grim look on her face that made the uncomfortable feeling in my chest tighten further.

Before she could get to me, the front door opened again, and that time a boatload of brothers came through. All of them seemed as though the weight of the world were riding on their shoulders. Shameless, Rabbit, Whiskey, and Fox all headed straight for the bar, taking no notice of me sitting over in the corner. Nor did they see Charlie, who had stopped mid-way to me so that she could see who had come through the door.

Panic set in immediately upon seeing Whiskey and Fox enter without Tango hot on their heels. I stood from where I'd been patiently awaiting news. Charlie glanced from the door to me and back again just in time for it to release once more with a hiss. In walked Tango, looking completely defeated, and my heart immediately elated and sank all at the same time. He was back and safe. That observation alone had my heart soaring, because I'd begun to think he hadn't made it back in one piece.

The look on his face, when his eyes found mine, told me this story was far from over and it wouldn't be pretty. I prepared myself for the fact that he was going to tell me he was turning me over to the KDMC on his club's orders. I was too much trouble, and I didn't blame them one bit.

Instead of going to the bar with all the other men, Tango headed straight for me. "Babe," he groaned, as if seeing me healed something that had broken inside him. His arms wrapped around my body and his head sank to the point where his forehead rested on the tender area between my shoulder and neck. "I don't know how to say this," he started as he squeezed me tighter to him.

"You're sending me to them," I whispered. "It's okay, I understand."

"Fuck no!" he admonished. "Not a damn soul here would do that to you." He pulled me back over to the couch I had so recently vacated. "I need you to sit down with me. I have a lot to say and not all of it is good news."

"Okay, can you just spit out the bad stuff now, because looking around at everyone is making me nervous. I thought they just didn't want to tell me anything because you were sending me away."

"The King's Demons had your brother," he blurted out as he took hold of my trembling hands. One word stuck out, because it was past tense. *Had.*

"Had?" I questioned, lip quivering.

"I brought him back with me," he stated as he glanced down shaking his head. "We didn't even get a chance to do anything. He was gone before..."

"Gone?" My voice cracked on the one word as I interrupted Tango. "My brother, he's gone?" His head tipped down slightly, almost a nod, indicating that I was correct. "You said you brought him back."

"I brought his body back, Liza. I couldn't leave him there to be swept up with the others when they cleaned up their mess."

"Others? I don't understand. You better start from the beginning."

He did just that, as he filled me in on exactly what transpired when they got to Casper, and about the carnage they left behind. He also fumed about not being the one to send the two bastards, who had hurt me when I was held captive, straight to hell. I only had one thing on my mind, though.

"Can I see him?"

"I'm not so sure that's a good idea, babe," he explained gently. "I brought him back, but he was in bad shape before they shot him. He, well, you won't be able to recognize him."

"He has a tattoo on his wrist. It's just four words, 'my life for hers' can I just see that much. I need to know for sure. I know you wouldn't lie to me, but I need to see for myself."

Tango nodded, stood, and pulled me up by our joined hands. My legs shook as I took that first step forward and he halted. He turned and moved as if he was going to pick me up, but I shook my head. There was no way I wouldn't walk on my own two feet to see my brother for the last time. I imagined that he'd taken a bullet rather than give up information about where I was.

He kept the promise he made me when he got that tattoo on his wrist. "Never again," he'd said as we strolled into the shop, and he had his buddy ink the words on his skin. "My life for yours," he told me as I read the words. "That's how it should have been from the beginning. I promise you, from here on out, that is how it will always be."

"He kept his promise," I stated as Tango moved me into the shed out back and pulled a cover up from the middle of the body shaped form that was laid out on the top of a workbench. He didn't find what he was looking for, so he moved to the other side of the table and then called me over. I took my time getting there; staring at the human shaped form that I knew was my brother's body. I tried to remind myself that it wasn't my brother any longer. It was simply the husk of his body that he had left behind when this world no longer needed him in it.

My heart physically hurt as I moved to stand beside Tango, who took my weight in his arms as he showed me the tattoo on my brother's wrist. That was when I knew it was true. My brother had died for me. He'd died for Michelle and the baby they'd made together. The same baby who would never be able to know their father. He died so that none of us would, but he also died because that dickhead Ransom couldn't just let things go. It was inevitably a pointless, unnecessary death. Now, I would have a job to do, because someone had to deliver the news to Michelle. I guessed I'd have to deliver his body to her, too. I didn't know. They hadn't been married even though I called her my sister-n-law.

My mundane thoughts were doing their job of keeping my brain occupied, but that only held out so long. Just as Tango and I were about to enter the clubhouse again, flashes of my brother's wrist hit me. He was truly gone. I had no one left outside of Michelle and the baby, and I wasn't so certain she would want anything to do with me again after all of this.

"What am I going to do?" The words were a whimpered plea and not much more. "I don't have anyone left now."

Tango stopped just as we cleared the door, and then he pointed me to face the room full of people who had apparently been awaiting our return. "You have so many people, baby. Look at them all." As he said that the hot tears won the battle and trailed hot rivers of anguish down my cheeks.

Before the first one fell, Charlie had me in her arms cooing sweet words in my ear.

"I'm your family now. Don't worry, I've got you," she told me as my body shook with emotion. Then another set of arms wrapped around both of us.

"Never had sisters before, but the two of you are everything. You will always have a brother here for you, sweetheart. I may not be the same, but I'll try damn hard to make you laugh every day and have your back always." Rabbit, who had become my surrogate brother through everything, squeezed me harder and let me cry it out on his shoulder until Tango gently guided me back into his arms.

He leaned in and whispered in my ear. "You hear that? You are not alone. You do not have to do this on your own, Liza. We are all here for you."

"Maybe you should take her upstairs," Charlie suggested when my body sagged heavily against Tango's. The grief was too much for me to bear alone. My brother had screwed up more than once, but he was still the boy who made me sandwiches when we were home alone because our parents were at work. He was the same big brother who walked me to school every day even though his school was two blocks closer than mine. He looked out for me my whole life before that big screw up when we were younger. He lost his life trying to look for me one more time.

A part of me wanted to be angry with Michelle for putting our family in this situation, but I couldn't because the heart wants what the heart wants. I knew that firsthand. Not only had my big brother kept me safe, but he delivered me into the arms of a surrogate family, too. I wondered if he knew that it would end this way.

Tango pulled me closer to the stairs, but before we moved to go up, I turned to the guys who were still gathered around watching us. "Thank you all," I started to say before I had to clear my throat as emotion choked me. "Thank you for taking me in and for going there today to deal with those monsters. It means everything to me that you all did that." I didn't have it in me to say anything more, and from the looks of the faces staring back at me, it had been enough anyway.

Once we were in the bedroom, Tango sat me down and took my boots off my feet. Then he pulled my socks off and continued like that until I was down to just my panties. He tucked me in bed under the covers and leaned in to place a gentle kiss on my forehead.

"I need to go get a shower and wash the road off me. You gonna be okay while I do that, or do you want me to call Charlie up here to sit with you?"

"I'll be fine," I stated with no emotion. It all seemed to have clogged up inside me somewhere. "I need to call Michelle. Does she know?"

Tango gave me a sympathetic look before nodding his head. "She was told just a little bit ago."

"Okay," I offered up a weak smile. "I should still call her, I think. See what she wants to do about..." I couldn't say his name, but I also couldn't call what was left of my brother 'the body'.

"Why don't you wait until I get back out here, and I'll sit with you while you make that call."

"Okay." I agreed as I felt the weight of the day pressing in on me.

TWO DAYS LATER, the men and women of the Aces High MC – Dakotas Chapter, and the visiting members who still hadn't gone home, all gathered with me out back where Tango set up a memorial service for my brother. Crusher and Van had taken the U-Haul the day before with my brother in it – inside a casket this time – to head back to Tallahassee where he would be received by my sister-n-law. She didn't want to go back to Reno, in case there were still any members of King's Demons or men who would suffer as a result of their sex trafficking ring being closed down for good.

I couldn't blame her. I didn't want to ever set foot in Reno again either. As a matter of fact, Tango had plans to go to Reno with Fox and Rabbit after everything settled down, to close down my brother's shop for him, and take care of packing his things up along with the rest of the stuff I'd left behind months ago.

I was touched that the club had put together a memorial of this caliber for my brother. I couldn't be there for the actual funeral that Michelle had planned, because the guys weren't completely sure that Guy, the National President of the King's Demons was on the up-and-up. They didn't want to take the chance of us leading them back to Michelle in Tallahassee just yet. Eventually, I'd be able to go visit, though probably not until after my niece or nephew was born.

We were standing by the table that had refreshments laid out on it, when the guys from Charleston walked up. "We just wanted to pass along our condolences again before we head out," Double-D told me.

"You guys are leaving?"

"Yeah, there's something going on with my youngest daughter. My wife told me to get my ass back yesterday."

"Well, what are you doing here? Get going! Your wife and daughter need you." Double-D grinned at me before glancing behind me at Tango who was positioned at my back.

"You got a keeper there, Brother. Don't let go of that."

"Don't intend to," Tango informed him.

"Let's get back," T-Bone finally told his dad. "Anna's never in trouble. I wonder what the hell she's done that has mom in a tizzy?"

"Don't know," he answered his son with a worried look on his handsome face. "Better get going so we can find out sooner rather than later though."

"Thank you, again, for coming here to help out with my problems."

Double-D offered up a brilliant flash of straight white teeth. "No need to thank us, honey, that's what family does."

His words hurt my heart even though that hadn't been his intention. My brother hadn't just sacrificed himself for me. He'd given me a place to be and people to love before he left, too. I wished I could see him one more time to tell him how proud I was of the man he had become. My anger was all gone now; replaced with the knowledge that he had put me in the best place I could possibly be to weather his loss.

After meeting the guys from Tallahassee, I had no doubt that Michelle was being well cared for too. It was something I planned to see for myself as soon as possible.

22. COMFORT AND KINDNESS

LIZA

"WHAT CAN I DO FOR YOU, BABE?"

"Just love me," I stated as he climbed in the bed and curled his naked body around mine.

"I already do love you." Tango brushed my hair aside and placed tantalizing kisses along my hairline at the nape of my neck. I immediately shivered as the euphoric feeling sent chills up and down my spine. "You want me lovin' you like this, or you need something more?"

"More," I panted huskily. My body had its own demands and apparently it was speaking for me.

Tango backed away momentarily before rolling me onto my back. He then climbed over top of me and leaned in to kiss my lips while probing my mouth gently with his tongue until I opened for him. We hadn't had the chance for intimacy since before he left for Casper, because there was just too much to do and too much sadness weighing me down besides. There was a bit of guilt too, because I could do this, and my brother would never get to be with his woman again. The flip side of my own argument was that he meant for me to be able to go on and live my life and be happy.

"Where'd you go babe?" Tango's smooth voice rolled over me in a low-level rumble that awoke my hunger for him once again.

"Sorry," I whispered. "I'm here, with you. Just reminded myself that it's okay to keep on living."

He made a weird noise before blanketing my entire body with his far larger one. "We don't have to do this," he stated as he moved to roll us both to the side facing one another.

"I want to." It was a simple statement followed by my lips tasting his, and me pushing my naked, warm body closer to him. I tossed my leg over his hip and opening me up to him. Tango wasted no time and immediately pushed inside. I wrapped myself around him, breasts squished into his inked up chest, left arm trapped beneath us, and my right moving its way up his backside as he pumped slowly in and out of me. We didn't have the best angle, but we had a level of intimacy in this position that I had never experienced with anyone before. I trailed my hand down his back once more feeling the muscles work as he moved himself inside my body. Once his taut ass was beneath my palm I squeezed and pulled, effectively signaling to him that I wanted to roll into a different position.

He obliged my needs, and moved with me, lifting my leg up into the cradle of his arm as he went. Tango, having a better position for it, started thrusting deeper into me. The man left me nearly breathless as he plunged in on a sharp down stroke and then pulled back out torturously slow. Each movement was a tease that took me closer to my release as he dragged back over that spot inside that demanded all the attention.

"T, I need…" I started to demand, but his mouth came back down on mine as he changed things up and swiveled his hips on the down stroke. When he pulled back from the kiss he was grinning like a loon.

"Do I have your attention now?" he asked as he did the hip swivel thing once again. I nodded my head enthusiastically which caused him to laugh. "Good."

No more words accompanied that one as he picked up the pace and began thrusting in and out of me in earnest. My hands found his smooth, hard glutes and held on as he brought me to the point of no return and thrust once more before tipping me over the edge. Tango followed behind me and the warmth that shot into my body was a reminder of the fact that we hadn't stopped to use protection.

"Shit," he hummed the word after he pulled his upper body slightly back from my own, so that he could look me in the eye. "I didn't use anything."

"It's okay. I don't think it's a particularly good time of the month for me to get pregnant."

"That may be, but I want to get tested so that you know you're safe."

"T, you already told me I'm the first woman you've had intercourse with in nearly three years. I'm pretty sure you would have fixed anything you had by now."

I was teasing him, but it was true. The man hadn't

indulged in that way, and I didn't think there was much danger from the few blow jobs he'd received either. If anything, he should be worried about me, because I'd had had one night stands here and there over the past couple of years. Not that I ever did so without protection, but still. "If it makes you feel better, we can both go this week."

"Yeah, we should do that, because babe, I never want to use a condom again with you. That felt incredible."

"Have you never?" I couldn't even finish the whole question, because jealousy kicked in and I didn't want to think about him being with another woman, let alone the fact that he was about to propose to one before.

"With Camilla," he confirmed quickly, probably sensing my discomfort.

"Oh," was all I could manage to get out before he hopped off the bed and headed toward the bathroom.

"Be right back," he announced. When he got back with a washcloth in hand, I let him know about my own history.

"I've never done been with anyone without protection," I admitted.

He smiled and went to work cleaning me up between my legs. A part of me wanted to be embarrassed to have a man cleaning me up in that way, but he'd been the one to make the mess, and in such a wonderful way that I couldn't complain or pull away from what he was doing, no matter my slight discomfort. When he was done, he tossed the rag on top of a small pile of clothes sitting off in the corner waiting to be laundered. Then Tango climbed in bed on the other side and pulled me to him so that my back was flush to his front.

"What the hell?" I giggled.

"I'm not lying in the wet spot, and neither are you. Lucky for us, the bed is plenty big enough and we can both fit on this side." I had to chuckle at that. It was sound logic, and something I hadn't thought of in my post bliss, worry-free moments.

"I don't know what I'm supposed to do now," I finally admitted to him. I felt Tango tense behind me.

"What do you mean?"

"I mean, I was brought here, and you guys were supposed to protect me, but I don't know where I fit now. Am I supposed to go back to Reno?"

"Do you want to?" His voice was thick with something left unsaid as he asked the question, so I turned to face him in order to see his reaction.

"I don't think I can ever go back there again." His hands started rubbing up and down along my back easing some of the worry and tension that had taken up residence there again so quickly.

"Then you don't have to. I don't want you to. Liza, I thought I'd made it clear that I wanted you to be mine, to be here, with me."

"I want that too, T. More than anything," I admitted before he leaned in and took my lips in his.

"That's settled then," he stated clearly. "I was going to ask if you wanted to head to Reno this week to help pack up Frankie's things," he informed me. "If you don't think you can do that, I'll go with Whiskey and Fox as planned." He thought about it for a minute and then changed his mind. "Better yet, I might see if Rabbit is able to go, instead. Whiskey and Fox still have their hands full with Amy.

"Are you sure it won't be too much of a bother to have you go that without me?"

"Are you kidding? No, it's not a bother, babe. The worst part of it will be leaving you behind when I go."

"Aww, I always thought the sweet-talk was supposed to end after you got me in bed," I teased.

Tango moved back just enough so that he could slap the top portion of my ass. "Yeah, well, I don't always do things the way everyone else does."

"Thank God for that," I mumbled causing him to laugh once more.

"Nah, more like, thank God for bringing you to me."

"Aww, T." I leaned in and took his mouth with my own. The man was just too much sometimes. My heart once again felt conflicted. Tango made me so unbelievably happy. Still, the death of my brother haunted me, and the sadness permeated. Sensing my mixed emotions Tango held me tighter.

"It's okay to miss him and be happy with your life all at the same time. He brought you here, to me, to my club, to this place where you found a new home. Celebrate that with his memory, babe. I think that's what he wanted for you all along."

Tears poured down my cheeks as he spoke, because it was the same thought that had kept me sane just days ago. My brother was never one to be mistaken for a psychic, but it seemed like he knew a little something in advance when he placed me in this situation with Tango.

"I'm in love with you," I finally told him while attempting to look him in the eye. That was made difficult by the tears that welled up and blurred my vision.

"That's good to hear, babe, because I am completely gone for you."

"What am I going to do now, though? I mean, besides staying here. I used to work for my brother when I wasn't doing graphic design jobs for businesses around Reno."

"I'm glad you asked, because I have been meaning to talk to you about coming to work for me. You can have the office in the back that isn't being used. When you're not working on the book covers or other design projects, you can help with tattoo designs. Only if you want," he made sure to specify.

I sat up a little then. "Seriously?"

"Yeah, babe. Kills two birds with one stone. You have a job and space to work, and I get to keep you close during the day, too."

"You're going to get sick of me," I stated.

"Nah, if I'm ever feeling like it's too crowded in there, I'll just shut the door to the office, bend you over the desk, and remind both of us why it's a great fuckin' idea." I laughed as I playfully smacked his chest.

"You are too much."

"Nah, babe. I'm just enough for you. That's all that matters."

"I can't argue with that." I didn't, in fact, argue with that. Instead, I leaned in and kissed him deeply. I wanted to commit the moment to memory and savor every juicy detail for the rest of my life. Tango was the man I had never dared to dream of, because I never thought my dreams deserved to come true. I still didn't think I'd earned him. Instead, I felt as though I was lucky enough to be just what he wanted and needed in the moment, and I was beyond okay with my lot in life. So long as my lot kept him coming back to me day and night, I'd have no complaints.

EPILOGUE 1
LIZA - 7 MONTHS LATER

As I GLANCED INTO TANGO'S EYES, I LOVED THE WAY THEY crinkled at the corners with his amusement. He knew I was up to no good. Hell, pretty much everyone who had spent time with me over the past seven months had gotten used to my bullshit.

"Just give it to me!" My voice came out in a weird mix of far-too-happy and whiney that made everyone around us dissolve into laughter. They all knew something was coming too.

"I don't trust you," Rabbit informed me.

"Mwah? Little old me?" I gasped in mock-horror at his revelation. "Why ever not?" I asked in an affected southern accent that was truly a horrible impersonation of Scarlett O'Hara from Gone with the Wind.

Rabbit quirked a brow and then grinned at me. "Frankly, my dear," he started, but then he couldn't hold a straight face either. "Fine! Go ahead and show me this fabulous thing you learned today."

"Yippee!" I shouted as I clapped my hands together while bouncing up and down on the stool in glee.

"Oh, you learned how to ride T's cock? Sweetheart, we all knew that. I think most of us heard you both earlier today." Rabbit winked at me while slinging a beer to Shameless who had to know he'd walked too far into the danger zone to back out now.

I narrowed my eyes on Rabbit. "I already knew how to do that just fine, thank you. Give me a cherry, a lime, two..." I stopped to think about it. "No, make that three pint glasses and two shot glasses." I did some fictitious math in my head and then smiled at the man who had become one of my best friends along with Charlie and a woman who danced at Renegade Rosy's named Cherry. Rabbit eyed me suspiciously once again, and then did as I asked.

I proceeded to set up the three pint glasses in a row, and then I placed the two shot glasses on top of the pint glasses, balancing them where the rims of the glasses were almost close enough to kiss one another. Then I took the lime wedge – a nice fat, juicy one – and the cherry. I popped the stemmed maraschino in my mouth, made a production of chewing it up and swallowing while still holding the lime all innocent-like.

Then, I asked Rabbit to spritz some soda into the glasses while avoiding the shot glasses on top since he had previously banned me from touching the spray nozzles for the soda and seltzer. He did as asked, and then poured some 151 Rum into the shot glasses on top when I directed him to do so. I teased Rabbit with a hint of cherry stem between my front teeth before I murmured one word. "Ready?"

He leaned in closer as I mirrored his action. While he was watching my mouth I reached over and squirted the lime right in his face before snatching a shot up, downing it, and then slamming one of the cokes back as a chaser. I shivered as Rabbit spewed and sputtered about his eye being on fire while everyone around us laughed.

"Damn boy, you never learn." Shameless chuckled as he grabbed his beer, took a sip, and started to walk off. Unfortunately, he was still in blast radius, and Rabbit pointed the spray nozzle toward the older brother.

"Neither do you, old man!" Rabbit called out, and just as Shameless glanced back he got a face full of seltzer. I continued to giggle until the hose was turned on me. It was fine though. I got the last laugh when Cherry's gorgeous twin sister, Chastity, strolled up to the bar about twenty minutes later, having just gotten to the clubhouse, and saw Rabbit with one red and irritated eye.

"Oh my God, Rabbit, what happened? You don't have pink eye, do you?" The woman took a healthy step back as if the man might have been carrying a deadly communicable disease instead of a possible pink eye infection.

"Poor Rabbit," I lamented with my lip poked out in a mock pout. "He learned a lesson about sniffing random panties and falling asleep with the wrong pair, didn't you, Captain Shit-Eye Willy?"

"Jesus," Tango muttered as he slid from his chair to come get me before Rabbit could fling himself over the bar to shut me up.

Chastity continued backing up even more.

Rabbit growled at me then as he pointed an accusatory

finger my way. "Paybacks are a bitch, woman! You remember that."

Chastity leaned in, then thought better of it and straightened back up. "Why? Were they her panties? You know she belongs to Tango, right?" Rabbit growled some more and said a few not so nice things about me under his breath.

I continued to giggle as Tango picked me up and slung me over his shoulder. It was a move my manly boyfriend seemed to enjoy. Not that I would ever complain because I loved when my man went all caveman on me. I still managed to see the smirk on Rabbit's face as he whispered something to Chastity. Well, he spoke low enough I couldn't hear, but she could still hear him from the safe distance she was maintaining.

"I can show you some videos online later about how to take care of all your princess parts so your panties aren't infecting the men," Chastity called out to me.

I huffed in indignation. "Don't you do his dirty work for him!"

"You were the one doing the dirty work, remember, sweetheart?" Rabbit called out his question on a cackle. "Maybe Tango can show you how to trim up and keep clean, so this never happens again." He pointed at his eye and poked his lip out as if he were going to cry. That bastard. "We need to protect the club members from your rogue dirty panties."

"You bastard!" I yelled from my position still flopped over Tango's shoulders as he moved up the steps bumping jostling me more with each step he took. "I'll squirt you in both eyes next time, but I'll use a lemon! Mark my... Ouch! Dammit, I was in the middle of making a point, T. My diabolical laugh was next and everything!" I pouted after Tango slapped the hell out of my ass to get me to shut the fuck up.

"I swear, you two are going to be the death of me," he lamented as he made it to our shared room and threw me down on our bed. We were still living together at the clubhouse. We were having a house built not far from the club. It bordered the property to the east, and until it was done, I didn't mind living amongst the guys. I was beginning to wonder how in the hell I was going to adjust to a quiet house once we eventually moved out. I was so used to the security here, and the noise of the men I had come to love and trust, that I wasn't sure how I would adjust to the quiet and lack of bodies willing to defend me if necessary.

Tango's phone rang, bringing me out of my thoughts. "Yeah? She did? Well shit, man. I'm happy for you guys! Yeah, I'm sure we will. We've both been drinking tonight, though." I continued to listen to the one-sided conversation as Tango devolved the conversation to grunts of acknowledgement and the occasional okay. When he hung up, his wary eyes captured mine.

"I know you don't want anything to do with Amy, but we really should go congratulate Whiskey and Fox on their baby girl."

"Of course, we can." I leaned into Tango and smiled into his chest thinking about the little bundle the boys had been blessed with. "Tell me about her," I stated before placing a kiss over his heart.

"She was seven pounds, three ounces, has little sprigs of bright red hair, and she came into this world screaming up a storm according to the guys. They named her Tori Ashlynn Waters."

"Aw, are we going to see her tomorrow?"

"In the morning, if you're okay with that?"

"Of course, I am. I can't wait to hold her!" I squealed the last sentence. I might have loathed Amy and her antics that didn't stop after her banishment from the clubhouse, but I couldn't wait to get my hands on that tiny little baby.

I didn't miss the funny look Tango gave me when I started gushing about snuggling up to her and smelling that new baby smell, and hearing her coo, and how I wanted to rock her to sleep and sing to her. Okay, so I may have caught baby fever, but I totally had it under control.

"Soon as the house is ready, babe!"

"What?" I asked, clueless.

"You, me, and a baby of our own."

"Oh!"

"Yeah, oh!" He moved over so that he was standing directly in front of me and placed his hands on my flat tummy then moved them out further into the space that was between us. I can't wait to be standing like this and still touching the belly that holds our baby. You're already gorgeous, that's just going to ramp you up beyond perfection."

"Well, hell, if you wanted into my pants, all you had to do was say so, T. I'm ready and willing, but you can keep the compliments coming anyway. I like them."

"But do you like the sound of us building a family together?" There was a slight hesitation in his question, and I relieved it with a smile and my promise.

"I promise you, as soon as the house is ready, I'll be ready, too."

EPILOGUE 2
TANGO

THE NEXT DAY, WE WENT TO THE HOSPITAL TO SEE THE GUYS AND their precious new daughter. They were in a special room reserved for mothers who had just given birth, but the mom was suspiciously absent when we walked inside.

"Where's Amy?" I asked the question right away, because if we were going to have any issues, I wanted to know up front, so I could get Liza out of there. She could see the baby another time when the guys took her home.

Whiskey hung his head, shaking it back and forth in disbelief. Fox was the one to speak up.

"She's gone. Took off as soon as they released her this morning. The little one gets one more day in the hospital for observation and then she gets to come home with us."

"Will Amy be heading there too, or did she decide to do it?"

"She did it, man." That was from Whiskey. "I can't believe she could look at this sweet little face and just walk away, but she did."

"She signed the papers, and everything?"

"Yeah, man. The club's lawyer was here to tidy it up and earlier."

"Can I see her?" Liza asked Whiskey in almost a whisper.

"You can hold her," he informed my woman as he stood from the chair he'd been occupying. "Wash your hands first, and no kissing on her face."

Liza smiled at him. "Aw, look at you already being the protective daddy. That's adorable." Liza washed up and then took the seat Whiskey had just vacated before holding her arms out to accept his daughter from him. I watched in awe as my woman cradled the infant in her arms like it was the most natural thing in the world to do. Then she grabbed a tiny little baby bottle that Whiskey handed her and started feeding the tiny little girl.

"Looks like Tori might have a cousin sometime soon," Fox teased. Fatherhood already looked good on him. His grumpy demeanor had sloughed off as he helped Whiskey prepare for their impending child. We all saw it happen; like this light switched on behind his eyes and suddenly he knew what happiness was. Most people wouldn't understand, because they already knew it wasn't his biological child, but that didn't matter to Fox. Tori was his daughter just as much as she was Whiskey's.

"What?" I finally asked, because it had just dawned on me what my buddy insinuated.

"I saw the way you were just watching Liza with Tori. It won't be long before she brings Tori's cousin into the world."

I chuckled lightly. "You're not wrong. I already told her as soon as the house is ready."

Fox nodded.

"So, she really signed away her rights?" I lowered my voice to ask the question again, because I didn't want to upset Whiskey any more than I already had.

Fox tipped his head toward the door, and reluctantly I followed. I stood at a point where I could see into the little window of the door. My eyes stayed glued to Liza as she took the bottle from the sleeping baby's mouth, and then leaned her up on her shoulder, cradling the baby's head that was wrapped in a pink cotton cap, and started patting her back in order to burp her.

"She's a natural," Fox said before I shifted and gave him my full attention.

"Yeah, it appears so." I pulled him in for a quick hug and whispered, "Congratulations," in his ear. He shook a little, so I knew he had a lot of pent-up emotion he was trying to stave off. "What happened, man?"

"When she ran off, after she was banned temporarily from the clubhouse, we found her and convinced her to keep the baby for us. We offered to pay her a stipend, get her through the pregnancy, and had papers drawn up then for her to sign away her rights to us."

"I remember."

"Well, over the past couple months she's been coming around more and more, because Whiskey kept requesting to see her. He couldn't get enough of feeling Tori moving in her mom's belly, you know?" The love that shown in Fox's eyes wasn't entirely for his daughter at that point. Even I couldn't deny it any longer. Not that I had been clueless all along, but I was now certain that while the guys had harbored strong feelings for Amy at one point, they were also in love with one another in a different way.

"We thought she was coming around and wanted to try to fix things between all of us. The doc said early on that he thought she was having a heightened, abnormal reaction to the hormones. I don't know what the fuck really happened. We thought it was all leveling out and that we'd be able to work through the bullshit. She flat out told Whiskey that she was only ever with us to get to you. Told him that we were both sick fucks, and that she wanted nothing to do with us or our demon spawn."

"Jesus, fuck! Seriously?"

"Yeah, man," Fox acknowledged. "It was twisted. It's like she's a completely different person to the one we all met and took in. I can't wrap my head around it."

"That's a lot to take in especially with having to worry about what she was doing while she was pregnant." I sighed. "So, what are you going to do?" Fox was quiet for a few moments as he watched Whiskey hovering over Liza and the baby. He turned to me after a moment and laid it all out there and waited on the judgment to come. I smiled as he spoke, trying to reassure him that I loved both of my friends, and that I'd have their backs, no matter what.

"We're going to carry on and raise our daughter together. When the time is right, maybe we'll find a woman of value who will take us for what we are already, a family." I reached over and pulled him in for another quick side hug.

"You know I'm here for the three of you whenever you need me." I tipped my chin over at the little window that gave us a sliver of a view into the room. "We better get back in there before my old lady steals your daughter." Fox chuckled, but I could already see Liza growing attached. "Keep that in mind, I meant what I said earlier. We're both here for you guys whenever you need someone, okay?"

"Yeah, I hear you, T." He clapped me on the back. "Come on, I can see Whiskey fidgeting. He wants our daughter back. Better go save him from himself and get you guys on your way so you can make a cousin for Tori sooner than later. What's the point in waiting? If you knock her up now the house will be ready before the baby gets here." He offered the suggestion with a wink before heading back into the room.

I stood there a moment longer, contemplating what he'd just said. There was a time when I was ready to write off my friends and any advice that they might try to offer me. I came to realize that people make mistakes, they grow, and sometimes, they have the best ideas. Damn if I wasn't about to put those ideas into action. I hoped Liza would forgive me for taking his advice. I'd been dying to see Liza grow round with our baby, and to experience what it felt like to see and feel our son or daughter growing inside of her, kicking, and coming into this world screaming their head off. I could picture it as if it were reality already. I was certain that Liza wouldn't mind after she got to hold baby Tori. No matter what, I'd make my woman happy right along with any children we were lucky enough to parent.

THE END

Thanks for reading Whiskey Tango Foxtrot, book #2 in the Aces High MC - Dakotas Series

Please read/review the book, as this is how other readers find the books you love.

Don't forget to check out the other books in the Aces High MC - Dakotas Series.

- Dancing with Danger
- The Restart and the Remedy

Don't forget to sign up for my newsletter, so you never miss a new release!

https://christineandanne.myflodesk.com/newsletter

ALSO BY CHRISTINE MICHELLE

CHRISTINE MICHELLE

Kings of Anarchy MC: New Mexico

Property of Bigfoot

Aces High MC – Dakotas

Dancing with Danger · Whiskey Tango Foxtrot · The Restart and the Remedy

Aces High MC – Charleston

The Other Princess · A Love So Hard · The Princess and the Prospect · The Killing Ride · A Twist of Fate · Everlasting · A Year and a Day ·The Broken Beginning – Part One ·The Broken Beginning – Part Two

Aces High MC – Tallahassee

Crushed

Aces High MC – Sierra High

Walker · Trouble

Aces High MC – Cedar Falls

Redemption Weather · Proven · Smoke and the Flame · Redemption Duet Box Set

S.H.E. MC

Angel Girl · JoJo · Keys

Robeson Family Novels (standalones)

The Forgotten Wife · When the Last Petal Falls · A Different Husband

Standalone Novels

The Groupie Journal

Letters to Lily

His Bittersweet Regret

Bad at Love

TFO

The Fortunate Ones

T.I.E. Series

The Infinite Something · The Infinite Beat

Valhalla Rising

Revived

Dark Leopards MC (paranormal)

Ridden by Darkness · The B Team

Mirage Island Mates

Into the Grasslands · Beyond the Grasslands

Seasons Pack Series

Winter Wolves

The Ancients Series

Shadows of the Ancients · Falling into the White · Branches of the Willow · Bound by the Moon

Vukodlak Brew Series

Entwined · Enraged

The Awakening Series

Birthrights · Revelations · Incarnations

Death Viewers

Breathless

Upper YA Titles

The Voodoo Follies (PNR)

Catch a Falling Star (Dystopian Romance)

ANNE STORM

Savage Vipers MC

Wait For Me · Devastate Me · Surprise Me · Baby Me

Loved for the Holidays

Cupid Broke My Heart · Ghosted by Texas · Resolving Rumors

Cheating Hearts Series

The Homewrecker's Fate · The Regrettable Mistake

ABOUT THE AUTHOR

Christine Michelle runs on coffee and giggles as she writes her angst-fueled romance stories (motorcycle club, rockstar, paranormal, college, & other contemporary as well as women's fiction and marriage in trouble novels).
She is a mom to four humans (2 girls, 2 boys – all grown now).
When she's not writing books, she enjoys reading, drawing, hiking, or feeding her soul with live music at concerts.
Christine is a traveler and has lived all over the USA (and

other parts of the world). She currently lives in San Antonio, Texas with her two fur babies.

**Universal links to everything
(website, social media, book links, and more)**
https://linktr.ee/christinemichelle

facebook.com/M00nlitDreams

instagram.com/christinemichelle_annestorm

tiktok.com/@christine.michelle.books